LIFE IN LAKETON
COLLECTION:
four novellas

Life in Laketon Collection
Ebook ISBN 978-1-989642-41-2
Print ISBN 978-1-989642-40-5

.

Individual stories available in ebook and print:
Back at You © 2019 ISBN 978-0-9920052-9-0
After #8 © 2019 ISBN 978-1-9990509-2-4
Chancey © 2022 ISBN 978-1-9990509-4-8
Wildfire © 2022 ISBN 978-1-989642-33-7

© Shawn L. Bird. 2023

.

This book uses Canadian spelling.

.

Lintusen Press
PO Box 10019
Salmon Arm, BC
Canada V1E 3B9

LIFE IN LAKETON COLLECTION:
four novellas

Back at You
After #8
Chancey
Wildfire

Shawn L. Bird

LINTUSEN PRESS

LIFE IN LAKETON 1

Back at You

SHAWN L. BIRD

~ 1 ~

"I'm not going to be there do it." I shouted as I slammed the door. "You can't make me!"

"Kieran!" Dad staggered into the doorway. "You get your lazy butt back here!"

Let him come. I pushed my dirt bike out of the shed and stomped hard on the kickstart. The bike revved to life with a grumbling thunder and I roared out of the yard and into the hills. My mind was racing. My father the jerk wanted me to sneak through a store window to steal stuff for him.

"SCUM!" I shouted to the trees as I geared up and headed up a steep hill.

I flew off a jump and landed hard on the back wheel.

In the tracks of dirt I could see the outline of what could be eyes and a mouth. I imagined it was my father's face and I spun in circles, sliding the back wheel across it over and over, obliterating him.

I revved the bike in satisfaction and flew out onto the trail again.

With luck, by the time I got home, my dad would be back on his way north and with even more luck, he wouldn't be back until next spring. In an ideal world, he'd never be back, but that would be good luck, and I never had good luck.

I was at the top of the hill now, and the lake spread out beneath me, like twinkling blue glass. A boat made a slice across the bay on the south end. It'd be nice to have a boat, but I'd have to pay for it with smiles, and even that was too expensive for me these days.

I pulled into my favourite spot and turned off the bike. My fury had died down a little, but I still wasn't safe to be around other humans. I was better off in the woods with the beasts.

Not that I'd see any beasts after roaring all over the mountain on the bike. The by-product of a two-stroke engine was noise loud enough to send every creature for miles into hiding.

I couldn't believe Dad. He came up with the stupidest crap. He thought it was okay to steal from Park's just because he thought Asians 'deserved what they got for coming to this country and stealing jobs.' Dad was an idiot. Parks had started a business in Laketon and employed people! Sara even worked there occasionally last summer, helping them stock shelves.

Sara.

Now that I'd refused to go along with his stupid plan, was he going to try to recruit Sara? I had been so angry, I'd just left without thinking about that. I'd left angry, but Dad had been angry, too. When he was angry, he got violent. I had left my mom and my sister defenceless when I'd run off.

I felt a jolt of panic. The hairs on my body started to stand up. Was it my fear for Mom and Sara causing this sensation? My whole body tensed as I strained my ears, staring around the clearing.

On the right, some bushes were moving. A branch snapped.

Something was coming.

I stomped on the kickstart and it sputtered, but didn't catch. The rustling in the underbrush stopped.

I stomped again, as adrenaline flooded through me. Nothing happened.

A snout pushed through the leaves and a black bear emerged, its head up, snuffling the air as it squinted.

I froze.

Black bears aren't usually aggressive. They are happy to ignore humans unless they're defending food or cubs.

It's strange how some creatures will defend their offspring to the death, and others will throw them into danger to save themselves.

I stepped down again on the kickstart, praying that the bike would start.

The bear peered near-sightedly in my direction.

My heart pounded as I stepped down again. This time the bike roared to life. The bear swung its head and stepped backwards. A squeal in the woods on the other side of the clearing made the bear spin around. My heart sank. That was a scared bear cub and I was between it and its mother.

With a grunt the mother rushed at me, huffing.

I couldn't flip the bike around to race away from the bear, so I pushed the bike toward it. Would the bear lash its claws at me as I rode past it? As I roared closer, the bear veered to my right. I passed it so closely that I could have plucked hairs off its coat with my fingers, if I'd been brave enough to lift them off my handle bars.

I followed the path down the mountain, sliding and jumping until I felt the tension leave me. My heart had been echoing in my ears all the way down the trail, but it had settled to a regular march instead of an arrhythmic gallop by the time I made it to the road.

When I pulled into our yard, Dad's truck was gone.

I pushed the bike into the shed and went into the house. Mom was sitting at the kitchen table nursing a cup of coffee.

She looked up as I came in. There was a swelling on her cheek and a wet cloth on the table.

I sighed. "He left you a good-bye present, I see."

She just tightened her lips. I went to the fridge, took out an ice cube, then I got out a clean dish cloth, bundled it around the ice, then whacked it hard on the counter. I found the mallet in the drawer and smashed the ice.

Mom winced at the noise, but when I handed her my make shift ice pack, she took it and set it gingerly over her swollen cheek.

I sat down at the table. "Where's Sara?"

"I sent her to Josie's house."

"Before or after?"

"Before. She didn't see it."

I nodded. My little sister did not need to see our dad beating on our mom. "I'm going to kill him some day."

Mom scowled, "No, you're not. You're not stupid enough to throw your life away after a drunk like him."

I wanted to argue, but 'Yes, I am stupid enough to do that' wasn't something I wanted to admit, even if I was failing all my grade nine classes.

"I thought when I divorced him we'd be done with this," she sighed.

"Are you going to tell the police?"

"Why bother? He's gone now."

"You know why."

She raised her eyebrows.

I sighed. "When I kill him, we'll need the paper trail to prove it was justifiable homicide."

"Don't even joke about stuff like that."

"Who's joking?"

She scowled at me again and glanced up to the clock. She set the cold pack on the table and stood up. "I should get started on dinner."

"No, sit down. I've got it."

"There's hamburger in the fridge. I was going to make a meatloaf." She said it as if it would be too much of a challenge for me.

"Okay," I said, rummaging for the meat, onions and celery.

"You're a good kid, Kieran. Thanks for doing this." She dropped her head on the table.

"You should go have a rest. Why don't you have a nap or something? I'll be fine."

"You're sure?"

"We made meatloaf in Home Ec."

"Aren't you failing Home Ec?" Her smile took the sting off her words.

I just laughed as I turned on the blender to puree the vegetables.

I'd taken cooking class at school because I was keen to eat. To my surprise, I liked it. It was fun to take a few ingredients and create something tasty.

I didn't cook often at home, but it was good to know I wouldn't starve if Mom finally got sick of me and kicked me out.

I dumped the pureed vegetables in to the frying pan to simmer while I dug my hands into the ground beef, mixing it with milk and egg. It was slimy and disgusting. That was another thing I like about cooking. It is totally gross, and yet the grossness becomes something wonderful.

Gravel crunched in the yard and I looked out the window the

see Dad's red truck was back.

I washed the meat off my hands, shut off the stove, and grabbed the baseball bat resting among the shoes at the back door.

~ 2 ~

I swung the bat back and forth as I sauntered down the sidewalk toward the shiny red pick up. The payments on that beast were eating Mom's child support. Dad was shutting the truck door.

I glared at him. "You're not welcome here. Get back in that truck and leave us alone."

Dad paused with his hand on the latch. "Kieran? Son? What's got into you?" He said it like he was a normal person.

Like I was the problem.

I glared at him, swinging the bat in a circle, arcing it high over my head. "I said, get back in the truck."

He didn't move. I swung the bat hard into the passenger side front fender. The crash reverberated up my arm.

"Hey! What the hell! This is a new..." He stepped toward me.

"GET BACK IN THE TRUCK!" I shouted, swinging the bat in a high slice. "I swear I will take your head right off your shoulders!"

He took a step backward, "Now, son..."

I slammed the bat down on the hood. The metal crackled as it caved. "Don't ever call me that!" I smashed the bat down again, deepening the concavity. "As of today, I am not your son!"

I could barely see him through the red haze that filled my vision. I spun the bat over my head and slashed it down.

Fury took me out of my body. I floated above him and watched his expression change as he saw the flash in my eyes. I saw the realization come to him that I could happily kill him, and he clambered backwards, into the truck. "Okay! Okay! I'm in!" He shut the door and glared at me.

"Leave town. Go up north and stay there. You are nothing like a father should be! You're a pathetic man. No real man would beat on his wife."

"I didn't mean to do it! If she didn't talk back…"

I slammed the bat into the driver's side door.

He winced and cowered, leaning into the middle of cab. Ducking his head, he turned the key in the ignition and the truck rumbled to life. "You need to grow up!" he shouted over the engine.

"Right back at you!" Grow up? That was rich. I spun on my heels and stomped into the house. My heart was pounding, and I thought my head would explode.

I collapsed into my chair at the table and put my head on my quivering arms. My legs were shaking.

Mom staggered down the stairs. A towel was wrapped around her and she clutched the ends in her fist. "God Kieran! What were you thinking!"

"I was thinking of getting him out of here."

"I thought you were going to kill him." Her face had drained of colour.

"Yeah. So did I for a while." I inhaled a shaky breath. "I should have."

She put her hand on my shoulder, "No, you shouldn't have. You scared me. I thought I was going to have to run naked into the yard to stop you. Never do that again."

"If he ever hits you again, I *will* bash in his head. I warned him."

She shook her head, closing her eyes and sighing deeply. "You're too young to be worried about this crap." She smelled of her fruity shampoo, fresh and youthful.

"I just want him to stay away, so we can have a regular life." I said, pushing the bat back into the closet and arranging the coats in front of it.

"Maybe he will now."

I could hear the sigh in her voice that meant she didn't really believe that.

I went back into the kitchen and finished making the meatloaf. I found a box of scalloped potato mix, I boiled the water, poured in the milk, put it into the oven as well.

I was just taking everything out of the oven when Sara came through the door.

Sara is twelve. She's one of those kids who wants so desperately to be cool that it's embarrassing. We don't have enough money for her to walk around in the most stylish clothes or anything. Around here, all the kids go to one elementary school and then move onto one high school. We've been with the same group of kids since kindergarten. People know you pretty well.

She sniffed, "That smells good. Did you make it?"

"I did."

She leaned over the pans on the cooling racks and inhaled. "Oh, that's heavenly. Are you trying to win points with Mom for some reason? Or is this to impress Dad?"

I chuckled, "No, impressing dad is not on my mind at the moment." The mixed vegetables had come to a boil, so I shut them off. "Would you set the table? It's all ready." I reached across her for the plates, as she gathered up the cutlery.

"Mom!" I shouted up the stairs.

"Only three plates?" Sara noticed my stack, and then glanced at the four settings she'd put out. "Is Daddy gone?"

I nodded.

She sighed. "Why is it that he never stays for very long? I'd like to spend more time with him."

"Go wash your hands," I said, as I brought the plates to the table. "We don't need him. He just hurts Mom."

She scowled. "No, he doesn't."

"Yes," I glared at her, "he does."

Mom came into the room, and Sara gasped at the sight of the puffy eye and cheek. There was a blue shadow around the eye. "Oh, Mom! What happened?"

"What do you think?" I snorted. "God, Sara."

"Sara, your father…"

Is a brute, and a terrible example! I thought. I set the plates on the table with a clatter. "Let's not talk about him. Enjoy your dinner."

Mom tilted the plate this way and that, smiling almost convincingly. "This looks lovely!"

Sara looked from me to Mom and back again. "Yeah. This looks really good, Kieran. Thanks for cooking."

Gravel crunched in the drive way.

I pushed my chair away from the table. "I'll get it." It was probably Dad again, and I wasn't going to let him have another shot at Mom or Sara.

I glanced out the window, but I didn't see Dad's now slightly beaten up new red truck in the yard. Instead, I saw the flashing blue and red lights of a police cruiser.

~ 3 ~

"Crap." I said.

"Kieran? Who is it?" Mom pushed her chair back.

The police weren't coming out of their car.

"It's just the police, Mom. No problem."

"Oh, no." She stood beside me and grabbed my arm. "What if your father is going to press charges?"

"Seriously?" I raised my eyebrows at her. "You just stand right here showing them your face and tell the police why I pounded on his truck. Just see what they do."

"Kieran, you threatened someone with a weapon!"

"I threatened the jerk who was beating up my mom. I kept him out of the house. I kept you safe. That's not an unreasonable thing."

Sara joined us, peeking through the curtains. "Why aren't they coming to the door? They're just sitting there."

We all stood there watching the car. My heart was pounding so hard I wondered if it was echoing out my ears. My temples were throbbing with it.

Another police car pulled into the yard.

"Why is there another one?" Sara squeaked.

That was practically the entire detachment in our driveway.

"What happened, Kieran? Are they going to arrest Daddy

for hitting Mommy?" Sara's quivery voice made her sound like she was five again.

I put my arm around her shoulders. "Dad's gone. They're probably here for me."

"Why?" she blinked up at me, and I squeezed her shoulders in a sideways hug. It showed how worried she was, that she didn't pull away.

Mom wrapped an arm around her on the other side and gave her a squeeze. "Never mind, honey. Go watch TV in my bedroom, why don't you?" Mom had a tiny twelve inch TV and a VCR in her room. We didn't have cable.

"No! I want to…"

"Sara," said Mom, in her no-nonsense voice.

Sara left, scowling and dragging her feet. "I'm too old for those baby videos!" she grumbled.

Two police officers stepped out of their vehicles and slammed the doors in perfect synchronicity. They walked together up to the door. When I heard their feet on the front porch, I opened it before they could knock. "Can I help you?"

One officer was a younger woman and the other was a guy with a pot belly.

"Good evening. I'm Corporal Fraser," said the pot bellied one. "This is Constable Hamilton. Is this the Smith residence?"

I thought about saying no, but I figured that was just asking for trouble. "Yeah. Is there a problem somewhere?"

"Well, yes. We had a report of a disturbance, so we are checking it out."

"Everything is quiet here, as you can see." Mom set her hand protectively on my shoulder.

The officers studied Mom's face, "Is that a new injury, Mrs. Smith?

"Yes."

"Did your son, do it?"

I laughed.

"Hush, Kieran."

Sara was making weird whimpering noises in the master bed room. I wondered if she was having flashbacks of the days before Dad moved out. She was pretty little, but even if she didn't remember consciously, I'll bet her subconscious was tuned into the screams that used wake her up at night. Sara'd start screaming, too, doors would slam, and occasionally Mom's body would slam up against a wall. Next there'd be flashing lights from the police cars lighting up the driveway.

"What kind of disturbance was reported, officers?" Mom asked. She was being absolutely polite, but her neck was flushing red, and her eyes were sparkling with tears she was keeping back.

We lived a ways from our neighbours. It'd take a lot of noise to disturb them. I looked at Mom to see if I could read what she was thinking.

"Was it a man?" I said bluntly. "Our only neighbours are women, and I doubt they can hear anything that happens at our house. My father, the jerk who gave her that black eye this afternoon, might have made the call on his way out of town, looking to make trouble."

They nodded with a professional detachment. "I see." Would your father have any reason to complain about your actions?"

Mom gave me a quick look.

I nodded. "He came back, and I told him to leave. He didn't want to. I was able to persuade him."

"How did you persuade him?"

"Maybe you should get a lawyer, Kieran?"

I narrowed my eyes and shook my head. "Maybe Dad should get a lawyer, Mom."

She looked at the two officers. "Is Kieran in trouble?"

"There are no charges against your son yet, ma'am." He turned to me. "Did you assault your father?"

"I hit his truck with a baseball bat." Best state it plainly. "I'm not proud of it, but he wasn't listening. He values the truck more than he values my mom. He beat Mom. I beat his truck."

"That probably wasn't the best way to handle the incident," Corporal Fraser said.

"If we'd called you, it would have taken you so long to get here that Mom could have been beaten to a bloody pile of bones."

"Kieran!"

"It's the truth, Mom, and you know it. If I hadn't made him go, who knows what would have happened. After he was through with you, maybe he'd hit me or Sara. Someone had to stand up, and you couldn't, so it had to be me."

The tears she'd been keeping back over-flowed, and she wiped them with the back of her hand, blinking.

"Thanks for your honestly, Kieran." Corporal Hamilton said. "I know how you feel, but next time, call us." She looked at Mom. "You may want to consider taking out a restraining order against your ex-husband. Then if comes on the property, you can call us immediately."

She shrugged. "That seems a little extreme. He's not really dangerous."

"Mom." I shook my head. "Have you *seen* your face? Anyone who can do that to someone as gentle as you is dangerous. It's not going to happen again. When I was little, I couldn't stand up to him, but now I can. I'm the man of the house, and damn it, he's not hurting anyone in my house!" I felt full of the fury again.

Not red furious, but steaming. My anger felt like a living thing, swelling and growing inside of me.

Corporal Fraser said, "That's *our* job, Kieran. You don't want to take the law into your own hands. You can end up getting yourself into trouble, even though your motivations are pure."

"Thank you for the warning."

"Thank you for your time. You take care of that cheek, Mrs Smith. Did you get photos of it?"

"I'll take some." I said. "Right, Mom?"

She nodded and wrapped a protective arm around my shoulder. As the police pulled out of the yard she murmured, "You need to be careful. They'll be watching you now."

I shrugged as we walked back into the living room.

Sara had snuck back and was sitting curled up on the couch, her eyes red with the quiet tears.

Mom squeaked in alarm, "Oh, Sar-Bear! Don't cry, honey. Everything is fine."

Sara shook her head and sniffled. "They were going to arrest Kieran!"

"Not this time," I said.

~ 4 ~

I had trouble sleeping that night.

I dreamt of Dad hammering on the windows, breaking down the door, attacking us all with axes.

I dreamt of him setting fires at the front and back doors to burn us alive.

I dreamt he was a vampire, and sucked us until we were dry and flat, like empty burlap sacks.

I dreamt of him stealing Sara and doing horrible things to her. I kept hearing Sara screaming in my dreams. Screams that made my blood turn to ice and then boil with fury.

Then I jolted awake because Sara really was screaming.

I threw back the covers of my bed and raced into her room. Flipping the light switch, I looked around frantically. No one was in the room with her. I sat on her bed, "Sara!" I shook her shoulder gently. "Sara! Wake up! It's okay. You're just having a nightmare! You're okay."

She shuddered into consciousness, wide eyed and gasping.

"You're all right, Sara." I repeated.

"He's not here?" she whispered.

"Dad?"

She nodded, gulping.

"No. You were dreaming. Can I get you a glass of water?"

She nodded, and I went to the kitchen. When I got back to her room with a covered coffee to-go cup full of water, Sara had crumpled back down onto her pillow, and was asleep again.

I sat down on the edge of her bed and looked at her. Little curls of hair stuck to her damp forehead. She was still just a kid. She didn't need to have terrors like this in her life.

I left the cup of water on her night table and went back up the hall. I stood outside Mom's room and listened. She should have woken up, like I did. Could Dad have gotten in and hurt her?

I slowly turned the knob and pushed the door open a crack. Mom was lying on her back, snoring lightly. She only snored if she'd taken a sleeping pill. Considering how badly my own attempts at sleep were going, I wished I had taken one myself. At least that explained why she hadn't heard Sara screaming. I shut her door softly and went to check the locks on the front and back doors.

I crawled back into bed. My old alarm clock said 3:17. It had been my grand-dad's clock. It had numbers made from little flaps that flipped over each minute with a funny, whirring click. I liked the sound. Usually it was a meditative kind of sound, lulling me to sleep. Tonight, each flip was echoing in my brain like an airplane taking off. School was going to come really early tomorrow. Or rather, today.

I closed my eyes, trying to lose myself in the clock's little mechanical meditation.

All too soon the alarm was making the grating electronic buzz that burrowed into my brain and rattled around until I could find the button to shut it off. For some reason I never could seem to find the right button in the morning. It would shut off, but three minutes later, it'd be screeching again.

I dragged myself out of bed and staggered down the hall.

Mom's bed room door was open. I listened to see if I could hear her rattling around in the kitchen, but all was quiet through the house. I remembered she was on the early shift at the dairy today. She would have had to be at work an hour ago.

I did my stuff in the bath room, and then knocked on Sara's door. "Get up, kid! You're burning daylight!" That was something grand-dad used to say.

Sara opened the door, blinking, with the glass of water in her hand. "Did you come into my room last night?"

"Yup. Do you remember your nightmare?"

She shook her head. "It's been ages since I had a nightmare. Did I wake you up?"

"Yeah, but don't worry. I don't sleep when fair maidens need defending from monsters."

She giggled and went into the bath room.

I got dressed and made breakfast. By the time Sara got to the table, I had toast, jam and juice out for her. She didn't look too much of a mess, and if she didn't remember her dream that was good.

Half an hour later, I was walking with Sara toward our schools, keeping a wary eye out for Dad's red truck. I was pretty sure he would have left town, but it'd be a week or so before I'd feel safe enough to let down my guard.

Sara saw her friends up ahead and waved good bye to me. Usually she was too cool to walk with me at all, let alone wave good bye, but then again, I usually didn't want to walk with her. Today I didn't want to let her out of my sight.

From behind me came a call, "Hey, Kieran!" I recognized Tom King's sneering voice. I kept walking, without glancing back.

Tom was the most irritating kind of bully. He was small. He

had a long pointy nose and beady eyes like a ferret. He always seemed to be lurking around corners and would appear out of nowhere to throw out a snotty remark. I was about a head taller than he was, and probably out weighed him by twenty pounds, but I always felt like I was a rat he was stepping on whenever he came around.

"I heard the police were out to arrest you last night," Tom caught up to me.

I shrugged and kept walking. It was best not to respond to him. He didn't need the ammunition.

"Your family are all useless. You're probably going to end up in jail."

"Oh?" I tried to laugh, because Mom said laughter diffuses bullies, but I could feel my skin tightening and all my nerves started tingling. "What for?"

"First, for being lazy and stupid," he said.

"That's two things," I said. "You can't even count. If lazy and stupid were crimes, they would have locked you up at birth."

Tom's eyes narrowed as he processed my insult. I shouldn't have said it, but I didn't care. I couldn't take crap from anyone today.

"We saw the police car. Were they arresting your Mom for running a brothel? Is she pimping out your sister?"

My vision changed, as the world took on a scarlet tinge. He wasn't just weaselly little Tom King. He was my dad. He was my impotence against my crappy life. He was everything I was mad at, and as I stepped toward him, I was going to pound him into the ground. I lunged at him. He swerved to his right, but I raised my left hand and powered an upper cut that slammed him beneath the chin. His head snapped back, and he dropped to the ground, gasping.

Blood oozed out of his mouth from a bloody tongue he kept sticking in and out, as he panted and gasped, the copper scent of it around him like an over-heated dog. Everything seemed to be painted red.

He was bleeding on the grass, blinking up at me with a stunned look, inhaling choppy breaths that didn't seem to be filling his lungs.

I felt a wave of dizziness and I shook my head, coming back to myself. "Crap." I said, looking around, as the other colours came back.

"I saw that!" an old lady shook her fist from her doorway. I called the police on you, Kieran Smith! I told them it was you!"

Small towns suck sometimes. Everyone knows your business.

"Call an ambulance!" I shouted to her. "He can't breathe!"

She hustled back into the house.

"It'll be okay," I said to Tom, "Mrs. Weber is calling for help.

He coughed another choking gasp in response. He was turning slightly grey.

"Here, sit up a bit, see if that helps you breathe."

What would happen if he died, right here? What if I'd crushed his trachea or something?

The change of angle seemed to make a difference. He sucked hungrily at the air, but at least he seemed to be getting some. For the moment.

"Just keep breathing."

Tom rolled his eyes. He opened his mouth as if he wanted to say something, but for once, he kept quiet. He shut his eyes instead, but his chest jerked up and down as he struggled to keep breathing.

I could hear sirens in the distance. That was it, then. I'd be hauled off to jail, Tom would die. I'd be a murderer.

Great. My dad was an abusive drunk, but perhaps I was a murderer. I had been so certain that I was going to be a better man than him, but I was worse.

Mom was going to be really ticked off with me now.

~ 5 ~

I stood there, staring down at Tom, trying to decide what to do.

I wanted to run.

I wanted to get home, climb on my dirt bike and ride up the mountain. I could take some food, find a cave, and stay away. I could live in the woods forever, and never have to face anyone. I could escape Dad. I could escape this.

Old Mrs. Weber was keeping watch over us, though. Her stare anchored me in place. Her ratty pink bath robe was illuminated by the morning light, so she looked like an avenging angel. She glowered at me, daring me to leave.

The dilemma was the same. If I left, who was going to protect Mom and Sara?

I just stood, watching Tom fighting to breathe, as the police car pulled up.

Officer Hamilton got out of the car and adjusted her utility belt. "What happened here, Kieran?"

I shrugged. "He needs an ambulance."

"One is coming." She knelt beside Tom. "Hang in there. Help is coming."

He nodded and winced, sputtering with pain. It seemed to me that he was struggling more than he had been before Constable

Hamilton showed up. Faker.

The ambulance arrived, and the officer pulled me off to the side. Mrs. Weber stomped down her walkway toward us. "I saw the whole thing, Officer. Tom and Kieran were walking along the street, and then Kieran punched him in the chin. He knocked Tom right out!"

"Ah ha." Constable Hamilton said, scribbling in her notebook. "Is that right, Kieran?"

I shrugged again. "He didn't lose consciousness or anything."

She slipped her hand cuffs off her belt. Suddenly I couldn't breathe, either.

"Give me your arms, please."

I stuck out my arms and the cold metal snapped around my wrists.

"Kieren Smith, I am arresting you for the assault of Tom King. Let's just sit you in the back of the car for a while. Watch your head." She guided me into the back seat.

The car smelled like plastic and cleaning fluid. I tilted my head back and rested it against the head rest. There were red dots splattered across the roof. The odour of cleaner was not quite masking something even nastier. The red dots on the roof wavered and I closed my eyes. I wondered how Mom would do if Dad came back while I was in jail. Sara wasn't going to be beating him off. Sara could barely lift the baseball bat.

There was a thump behind me and I looked out the window to see that the paramedics had Tom on a gurney and were loading him into the back of the ambulance. There was a plastic mask over his face, and tubes coming out of his arms.

Constable Hamilton was still talking to Mrs. Weber on the front step. I closed my eyes again. My mom was going to be so freaked out about this.

How could I have let my temper take over again?

The ambulance siren started up and it headed toward the highway. Constabe Hamilton opened the driver's door. "All right, back there?"

"Yes, ma'am."

"Okay then. Off we go to the station."

My heart started thudding again. This was it. I was going to rot in jail. My life was over. I tapped on the divider between the front and back seats. "How's Tom? Is he going to be okay?" *Was there any hope?*

Constable Hamilton shook her head. "I don't know. It's very serious, for sure."

The station was only a few blocks away, of course. Everything was only a few blocks away in Laketon. She opened the garage door and drove in. She opened the back door and guided me out. It'd been about fifteen minutes, but already my wrists burned and my arms ached from the cuffs.

"Come along through here, please."

She opened a door and led me down a hallway and into a little room. "Have a seat." I went in and sat at the little table. "I'll be with you shortly."

The room was not much bigger than a small bath room. The walls were a pukey grey green. There was a small window in the door. The fluorescent light in the ceiling buzzed. It seemed to get louder as I sat there. Every so often it flickered. It made my head hurt. I folded my arms on the table and set my head on it. Suddenly I wanted nothing more than the oblivion of sleep. I didn't want to face any of this. I think I actually did fall asleep for a while. My brain just shut down and saved me from thinking about anything, but I dreamt again of Dad breaking into our house, hurting Mom, hurting Sara, but this time I was on the outside of barred windows, hammering to come in, while he looked up at me and laughed.

~ 6 ~

Constable Hamilton came in holding a cup of coffee and a bottle of water. I blinked up at her. She passed me the water, as she took a sip of her coffee and sat down. She had a phone and a note book.

"Kieran, I am required by law to ask you if you would like to speak to your parents, and whether you want legal counsel."

I shook my head, "We can't afford a lawyer."

"How old are you?"

"Fourteen." Fourteen and my life is already over because I've probably killed someone, I thought.

"There is no charge for a lawyer for youth. Do you know anyone?"

I shook my head again. "I don't want to talk to anyone."

"Are you declining legal counsel?"

"I don't want anyone to know. Not my mom, or dad, or my sister. I don't want to be here." To my supreme embarrassment, my eyes brimmed with tears.

"Sorry, kiddo. That's not the way it works. Besides, you know that there was a witness. Mrs. Weber will probably have the news all over town within the hour."

I sighed. She was right. There was no anonymity in a small town. It would be horrible if my mom heard I'd been arrested from someone else. What a pathetic loser son I was. I put my head back down on my arms. How was I going to tell her? I looked up at the officer. "What should I tell my mom?"

"To come here, maybe?"

"Oh. Yeah." She handed me the phone and I dialled the dairy. Normally Mom couldn't take calls there. When someone finally picked up at the ice cream store, and I asked for mom, they told me she wasn't available. "It's an emergency. Can you please tell her to call Kieran at this number?" I read the number from the back of the phone.

"Isn't that the non-emergency number of the police station?" the woman said.

I inhaled deeply and counted to five slowly, trying not to curse living in a town so small that everyone knows all the contact numbers off by heart. "Yes." I said, finally.

"Just a moment, please." I could hear her shouting at her colleagues, "Kieran's at the police station. Someone find Meghan, she needs to come to the phone!"

It seemed like forever before I heard, "Kieran? What's wrong? Are you okay? Is Sara okay?"

"Sara's at school. I'm sure she's fine. I need you to come to the police station, though. As soon as possible."

"Why?" an anxious tone had replaced the frantic one of a moment ago.

"I've been arrested. Can you come?"

"I'll be right there." she said with clipped tones as she hung up.

I handed back the phone, but Constable Hamilton waved her hand. "Were you going to call a lawyer?"

"I don't know any lawyers."

She pushed a paper across the table. "Here's the list of who's accepting clients at the moment. Call any of them."

There were five names. I closed my eyes and stabbed my finger down. When I opened my eyes, my finger was pointing to John Malcolm. "I'll call him. Will he come right away?"

Constable Hamilton laughed. "Good heavens, no. The lawyers are far too busy to leave their offices for a consultation. He'll talk to you by phone and give you the initial advice."

I dialled and asked the receptionist if I could speak to Mr. Malcolm.

"What is this in regards to?" she asked in a bored monotone. I could almost see her at a polished mahogany desk sitting in her comfortable black leather chair, guarding Mr. Malcolm from the riff-raff of society. Riff-raff like me. Well, he needed us riff-raff to do his job, didn't he? Constable Hamilton stepped out of the interview room, to give me privacy. I thought that was nice.

"I'm in jail. I need a lawyer. I'm fourteen."

She sighed as she said Mr. Malcolm would be with me in a moment.

When he came onto the phone, I told him where I was. "I hit a kid. They took him to hospital."

"Did you tell the police that?"

"No. A lady saw me. She told Constable Hamilton"

"You're sure you haven't said anything to them? Did you apologize or anything like that?"

"No. I didn't say anything."

"That's good, kid. That's the most important thing. You don't make a statement. You don't admit to anything."

"He was lying on the ground, having trouble breathing. They know I did it. I know I did it. Why should I lie about it?"

"You don't lie about your actions, either. You don't say anything. If they ask for a statement, you say, 'My counsel has advised me not to make a statement at this time.'"

"That's it?"

"That's it for now. Have you called your parents?"

"Yeah. My Mom is coming."

"Good. Don't let her say anything, and don't let her pressure you into saying anything, either. This is about legalities. Don't say *anything*. No statement. Got it?"

"All right. Thank you."

I rested my head back on my arms and closed my eyes. I was an expert at saying nothing. Sometimes at school I went a week without saying a word to anyone. That might be the easiest instruction I'd ever been given.

There was a knock at the door and Mom flew in. "Oh, Kieran! What did you do?"

I waited for the door to close, with Constable Hamilton on the other side of it, before I responded. I told her everything. There was no point hiding anything from Mom. Mrs. Weber would be spreading the story everywhere she went today. Mom needed to learn everything from me.

"Oh, Kieran," she said, and she sniffed like she was trying not to cry. You have to tell them everything. Be completely frank and open."

"No. The lawyer said not to give a statement."

"Did you ask how much the lawyer charges?" she gulped.

"He's free because I'm a kid."

She exhaled. "Oh. Right. That's good."

"He said that the witness will tell what she saw and that's enough. I shouldn't say anything."

"Surely Mrs. Weber is not going to have a correct interpretation on the situation. You have to tell them your perspective!"

I loved my mom, and I usually respected her advice, but somehow this time I wasn't going to risk her judgement. She wasn't making the best decisions lately. She'd let Dad back into the house, after all.

"You should have charged Dad with assault when he hit you. If you had, maybe I wouldn't have been so angry that I hit Tom."

She just stared at me and her eyes filled with tears.

I closed my eyes and thunked my head on the desk. I knew that wasn't fair.

The fist was attached my arm, not hers.

Clearly, she didn't always make the best choices, but I hadn't either. This time, I was going to listen to someone with experience dealing with idiots like me.

"I'm sorry. I shouldn't have said that."

Mom gave a quivering breath and nodded.

Constable Hamilton came into the interview room. She opened her little notebook and set a small audio recorder on the table. "All right, Kieran. Now that your mom is here, are you ready to make a statement about what happened this morning?"

She looked expectantly at Mom and then smiled at me, as if to assure me that it was all going to work out beautifully.

I shook my head.

"Kieran?" Mom nudged, "Tell Constable Hamilton what happened, honey."

"No." I tried to remember what John Malcolm had said. "My counsel has advised me against making a statement at this time."

"Kieran!" I don't know why Mom looked so shocked. I had just told her that's what he'd said I should do. "You have to tell the officers what happened!"

I shook my head again. "No, I don't. I am not making a

statement." I gave a chin flick toward the recorder. "You can turn that off. I'm not going to be saying anything."

Constable Hamilton sighed. "You're sure?"

"I'm sure. Do you take me to jail now?"

She smiled faintly. "No. I issue you an 'under-taking to appear.'"

"Huh?"

Her lips quirked up as she explained, "It's a bail order."

"We can't afford to pay bail," I sighed. Just lock me up. At least Mom won't have to pay for my groceries while I'm in jail.

She shook her head and smiled. "You don't have to pay anything. You just have to promise that you will be appear in court."

"I can do that."

"I know. But there are conditions. First, you can have no contact with Tom, either directly in person, or indirectly through social media."

"How am I going to avoid contact with him?" I asked. We go to the same school. We're in the same classes."

"Yes. We'll see how it goes. The order says, "'except for incidental contact while attending school.' We'll see how it works. If you both behave yourselves, that will probably be fine. We'll work it out with your principal."

"Okay. What's next?"

"The second condition is that you have to stay away from his house."

"No problem. I never go near his house."

"Good. Third thing is that you can't have any weapons on your person."

"I don't carry knives or guns!" I grumbled. She was making me sound like a felon. I thought about that for a moment. I had been arrested. I was sitting in a police station. I *was* a felon. The thought made my stomach heave. Somewhat shakily I asked, "Is that it?"

"One more. The final condition is that you're going to have to meet regularly with a youth bail officer."

"A what?"

"That's just the other name for a Youth Probation Officer. Your order says you'll meet with him weekly for now. Your officer is Rob Sky. He'll call and arrange where he'll meet you."

Mom just sat in the corner listening with a stream of tears coming down her cheeks. "Sign it, Kieran. Let's get out of here."

And that was it. I signed, and I got to walk out of the police station. I couldn't believe it. I had been so sure I was going to jail. I stepped out into the sunshine and felt incredibly thankful. I knew I was lucky. I had screwed up, but a lot of eyes were going to be watching me now. I couldn't mess up again.

Mom walked us to the car and I slipped silently in beside her. Her eyes were red rimmed. She kept glancing over to me, as if she had something important that she wanted to say, but I didn't meet her eyes, and she didn't seem to get the courage to say whatever was on her mind.

We turned left as we left the station. "Wait. Aren't you taking me to school?"

She raised an eyebrow. "Not today. Today you're going home, and you're going to figure out what happened to you, and what you're going to change to make sure it never happens again."

"I want to go to school."

She pulled into our driveway and shut off the ignition. "I can't deal with this, Kieran." She turned to me, putting her hand over the seat belt buckle so I couldn't release it and get out of the car. "I can't have my son beating people up and getting hauled to the police station. You understand? I went through that with your father. Look what he turned into."

"I am not my father!" Bile rose up the back of my throat at her implication.

"I hope not, but this is exactly how he started: getting drunk and beating up other kids at parties."

"I wasn't drunk and I wasn't at a party. I was walking down the street on the way to school minding my own business."

"That makes it worse. At least your father always had an excuse."

"That's a cop out. How could you have fallen for that?"

She shrugged, "He loved me. We were childhood sweethearts. He was all I knew love was. Punching people isn't love, though."

"That's what I've been telling you. Why are you lecturing *me*?"

Her eyes actually darkened as she looked at me. "Kieren," she said in that freaky no-nonsense mom voice, "Lack of self-control isn't cool. It's pathetic, and you need to get control of yourself. You can not become your father."

"I won't!" I slammed my hands into the dashboard. The pain zapped through me.

"Kieran. That's enough."

I shook my head. "I will *never* become like him." I blinked at the tears that were burning my eyes, and I noticed the expression on her face: fear. "I love you and Sara. I don't want to hurt you! I will never hit either of *you*. You don't have to be afraid of me."

"Your father said that to me while we were dating." In response to my scowl, she gathered me up into her arms and rocked me in her tight hug. "I know you wouldn't ever mean to, but there are other ways to hurt us. I love you, Kieran." She pulled back and set a hand on either cheek. She stared into my eyes. "I know you can be a better man than this."

"I will be," I sniffed. I meant it. I wasn't going to be like my dad. "What are we going to tell Sara?"

"As little as possible. She doesn't have to know about the

probation order or any of that. She'll hear that you hit Tom." She rolled her eyes, "This is Laketon. She probably already has, but we'll try to protect her from the rest."

I nodded. I wasn't sure it was the best plan, but it'd do for now. If we could pretend things were normal, maybe they would be.

That night, Sara didn't ask any questions. We made dinner together, and she chattered about a class project they were doing and giggled about a boy she had a crush on: one of the hockey players who had just joined the team. She'd gone to practice with some of her friends and watched him play.

"You should see him, Kieran. He is so dreamy!"

I rolled my eyes at that. All the girls crushed on hockey players at one point or another. I let her talk, and when her words started blending together, I stretched and yawned. "Good night, you two. I'm going to bed early." I was surprisingly tired.

I was nervous going to school the next day. I knew that the principal, Mrs. Sykes, would have heard about what happened. I was even more sure that she'd want to see me and decide whether someone failing everything like me should stay in school, if he was a danger to someone like Tom King, who was our basketball high point man, and who generally had A's.

The more I thought about it, the more I knew she would pick Tom and send me packing. Rather than wait for her to page me out of class and have the whole school know that I was getting kicked out, I went straight into the office when I got to school. If she kicked me out before school started, nobody even had to know I'd been here.

Mrs. Sykes was standing chatting with the secretary, but she looked up as the door closed behind me. "Ah. Kieran. Just who

I wanted to see. Can you come into my office, please?"

I followed her in and sat on the blue plastic chair, bouncing a foot up and down to channel my nervousness as she settled down behind her desk in her big comfortable principal chair. "So." She lifted a wad of papers. "I have a copy of your Order here. You got yourself into some trouble, didn't you?"

"Yes, ma'am." I didn't meet her eyes.

"I was surprised to hear about the incident. At present the condition that you not to have any contact with Tom is quite simple to follow, since he's still in the hospital."

I snapped to attention. "He is?"

"Have you heard anything about him?" she asked, catching my expression.

"Nothing since they wheeled him into the ambulance. Is he going to be okay?"

"He was hurt badly, Kieran. He is still having difficulty breathing because of the swelling in his throat, and he's not talking yet. You'll have to pray he recovers."

I nodded. Injured was better than dead, but neither was very good when you were the one responsible for it. If something bad happened—like he never got his voice back, or his throat swelled so much that he suffocated to death—I couldn't see them letting me wander around town on a 'agreement to appear.' "I hope he gets better soon," I said sincerely.

"Me, too. In the meantime, there are some expectations on you."

"I know."

"Your probation officer will be here later this afternoon to meet with you. We'll page you when he comes."

She stood up and stood at her door. "I expect you to work very hard to make this work, Kieran. Keep out of trouble. Get

~ 45 ~

your school work done."

I stood up. "Yes, ma'am."

The bell rang, and I headed down the hall to class. It felt so weird. On the surface, nothing was different from any other school day, but my whole life had changed

~ 8 ~

At first, it wasn't too bad. I met with Rob, and it was fine. He talked about my family, my anger, what I'd done, and set me up with an anger management counsellor. Mom didn't have to pay for anything, since he wrote that it was a condition of my restitution. That was good, because she wouldn't have been able to pay for it. We had to go to the Food Bank that month as it was.

Ten days after the attack, Tom was back at school. He was pale and sickly looking, but when he came into Science class, he met my eyes with a glare that dared me to come at him again.

His friend Chris strolled across the class. "We're watching you, Smith. I would watch my back if I were you."

I quirked a brow. "Back at you." I turned away from him and took my seat on the north row. Tom settled at the south edge. He narrowed his eyes and drew a finger across his throat.

I smirked at him like I thought he was funny. Inside, my stomach churned. I wanted to punch him again. Despite everything, I wanted nothing more than to shut him up with my fist.

I was not going to come at him at school, of course. I wasn't allowed to talk to him. Ms. Wilson had moved my desk to the opposite side of the room from Tom's and for our group project, I was obviously in a different group from him. It was no big deal to avoid him.

I didn't want any trouble, after all.

But apparently Tom did.

It was subtle at first.

He'd pass me in the hall and jostle my shoulder.

A paper airplane fired into the back of my head. Chris whispered, "Watching your back?" as he went by.

In PE, Tom threw the dodge ball at my head. Chris raced across the room and 'accidentally' ran into my knees.

In science class, fluid appeared on my desk.

In English, my text book suddenly disappeared from my desk, and showed up in the garbage can at the door.

Each little annoyance was meant to make me get mad enough to react. They were trying to get me to break my conditions.

Every time, I counted to ten, cleaned up, gathered my materials, and did my best to ignore him.

At our probation meeting I told Rob, "He's deliberately trying to get me to react."

He nodded and tapped his pen on his notebook. "What strategies are you using to make sure you don't?"

I told him. I was counting until I calmed down. I was leaving the room. I was ignoring it.

"That's good. Just keep doing that."

"Easier said than done," I muttered. "I feel like I'm in a pressure cooker. I can feel the steam building."

Rob nodded. "I understand. It's important that you continue to ignore the provocations."

"They're all watching me. They don't see anything he does. I'm the perpetrator who hurt poor Tom. He's the innocent victim." I glared at Rob, "He isn't innocent. He's a bully. That's why I hit him."

"Keep up the good work," Rob said, packing the papers into his briefcase. "I know it seems unfair, but we'll keep documenting any issues in case there's trouble later."

I sat in the little office we used for our appointments after he left. We didn't need to wait for trouble later. Tom was trouble now. I didn't like being played. My father played these kinds of games. I'd had enough experience with my dad that I should be a gamemaster by now. Unfortunately, when the red filled my vision, all bets were off. So far, so good. If I could help it, I wasn't going to breech my probation and risk ending up in a youth detention facility. I couldn't. Mom and Sara needed me.

~ 9 ~

It was after school on Friday. I was walking home thinking about Sara and Number Eight, her hockey player crush. It was kind of creepy how girls get when they've got a crush on someone. I don't remember any girls crushing on me, but maybe it's hard to tell unless you're around them all the time? More likely no one has ever had a crush on me. Sara had friends who giggled around me, but I'd known them since kindergarten. I couldn't imagine them have romantic day dreams about me. Gross.

I liked a lot of girls I'd met on the beach. That's the best thing about living in a small tourist town like Laketon: girls who come here on their summer vacations. They hang out on the beach and flirt with us, because they want a summer romance. A week, maybe two and they're gone, but they could be fun while they were around.

The girls in my class weren't interested in me. I was always too boring. Now I had a reputation. I was *dangerous*. Maybe that would make me more interesting? I was chuckling to myself when a rock rolled past my feet, a few steps ahead.

My heart thudded, but I didn't give in the urge to look behind me. I faced forward. I quit day-dreaming though, and started paying attention for more signs of trouble. Branches were creaking. A car door slammed down the road. Someone was laughing at someone. The train was heading over the bridge in the distance. There were steps behind me.

I didn't dare turn around.

I started walking a little faster, wishing I had some weapon on me to defend myself if they jumped me. Then I remembered. No weapons. I wasn't allowed to defend myself. A stick. I wished I had a stick. I glanced into the woods. Maybe I could find something in there.

A whining whisper came out of the trees on my right, "Kierrrrrran..." It made the hair rise all over my body. My heart started to beat like the drummer in a rock band.

The whisper was echoed on my left, "Kierrrrrran..." I swallowed and walked faster. If I broke out into a run, I had no doubt that they would start chasing me. Right now, they were just trying to scare me.

It was working. It's amazing how scary it is, just to hear someone saying nothing more than your name under those circumstances.

I rounded the corner and there was Tom, standing in the middle of the road.

"Hello, Kieran," he croaked. His voice was still hoarse from the damage my punch had caused.

"I'm not allowed to talk to you, Tom. You know that."

"You'll have to get around me," he hissed.

"I don't want trouble. Let me by, please."

He smiled. At least, at some level it was a smile, because his lips turned up a bit, but his eyes glared at me so malevolently, that it wasn't really a smile at all. He was goading me. I didn't want to fall for his game.

A couple came out of their house, their dog straining on a

leash, eager for its walk. Even out of uniform I recognized the woman. "Constable Hamilton! Good to see you!" I sprinted past Tom and attached myself to her side.

"I know you're off duty," I whispered, "but you just saved me."

"Oh?" she glanced back at Tom and frowned. "You're not supposed to go near him."

"I know. Tell *him*!"

She frowned again. "Where's your house again?"

I waved my arm, "A few blocks that way."

"How convenient," she said with a glance to her husband. "We were heading in that direction. Would you like to walk with us?"

I nodded. "Thanks. What's your dog's name?"

It was called Lacey and it was delighted to have someone new to escort it around the neighbourhood.

Constable Hamilton flicked her head back, to indicate Tom's gang casually strolling behind us. "Has that happened before?"

"No. He just got back to school today."

"You need to tell Mrs. Sykes and your probation officer. You have to document this kind of thing, for your own protection."

"I know. I will," I said. "He's been doing little things at school. No one else sees, though. He's a sneaky rat." We had reached my drive way. "This is my house. Thanks for the escort."

She nodded. "No problem. You just stay out of trouble, eh?"

"I'm trying," I said, as I pushed open the back door. Inside, I leaned on it and breathed deeply. That had been much too close. Tom and his friends could have jumped me. What would I have been able to do? I would have been the one in the hospital. In their twisted minds it would be perfectly okay to manipulate things so I did what they wanted. The wanted me to get into trouble.

~10~

"What's wrong?" Sara's voice made me jump in surprise as I came into the kitchen.

She set her glass of milk on the counter and studied me. "Something happened. What was it?"

"Nothing you need to worry about."

"Does it have to do with Tom bullying you?"

"How did you hear about that?"

She rolled her eyes. "How stupid would I have to be not to know about that? You could have told me, you know. I sounded like an idiot when kids were talking about it and I didn't know anything." She tried to look mad, screwing up her face in a glare, but she just looked like a mutant squirrel. "Everyone is still talking about it. You're the big news."

"Great."

"So?"

"What?"

She punched me lightly in the arm. "Is that what's wrong?"

I sighed. The way she was going, she'd have it all figured out soon enough. "Yeah. Kind of."

"Tom King is a total bully. He beat up Dani's brother."

That was news. "When?"

She shrugged. "At the start of school. She said Mikey was

just walking home, and Tom started saying mean things about her."

It sounded like Tom had a regular pattern of abusing little sisters. "So Mikey hit him?"

"Yeah, I guess. They had a fight. Neither of them had to go to the police station though." She looked at me pointedly. "Not like you."

"How did you know about that I went to the police station?"

"You know everyone finds out everything in Laketon. It is impossible to have secrets here. I would have thought you understood that."

I nodded. "I just thought…"

"I know. You and Mom were trying to protect me, right? You must think I'm completely stupid."

The phone rang. I picked it up without glancing at the call display. "Hello?"

"Kierrrrrrran…" said a spooky deep whisper. "You're going to hurt. Do you hear me, Kierrrrrrran?"

A shudder ran up my spine and I smashed the receiver down.

Sara grabbed my hand. "What was that?"

"Nothing. I need to get upstairs."

"Nothing like Tom is nothing? Come on, Kieran. Tell me the truth. I'm not a little kid anymore, you know."

"Sure you are. You're twelve."

"Twelve is old enough to get married and start having kids in some places."

I stared at her with my mouth hanging open. "What are you talking about? Twelve year olds are illegal child brides. You understand that, don't you?"

She shrugged. "Come on. Let's go get a milk shake at Maggie's. I have babysitting money. I'll treat."

Sara never treated. Sara was a princess, and she didn't share. She must feel really sorry for me to volunteer to buy milkshakes. "All right. Let's go."

I don't know what I was thinking. After the freaky voices in the bushes and a crank caller, you'd think I'd have the sense to stay inside. What can I say? I am stupid.

Stupid, but I *really* like milk shakes.

We had been walking about five minutes when I heard the first voice.

"Kierrrrrrrran…"

I ignored it, but I sped up.

"Slow down! What are you doing?"

"Hurry up, Sara."

"Kierrrrrran…" the voice said again.

Sara slowed and looked around. "What was that?"

"Nothing." I grabbed her arm and tugged. "Come on. Keep walking."

A rock flew out of the bushes and crashed into my knee.

"Damn!" I hopped a moment on one foot.

Sara stared at the rock. It was the size of my fist. "What the heck?"

"Never mind. Come on."

Another rock came at us. This time it hit Sara in the shoulder. She grabbed the spot and howled, "GET LOST, IDIOTS!"

"Sara!" I pulled on her arm. "Come on! Run!"

We ran. Another rock flew and hit me in the back. Then one hit Sara in the head. She dropped from a run to the ground in one move.

I saw red. In an instant I went from fearful and aware to vision filled with blood. "Get out here, you cowards! You want to fight? I'll fight! Leave my sister alone!"

The trees were filled with laughter. I bent over Sara. She was lying on the grass, groaning, and holding the back of her head. "Are you okay?"

"I never knew that I was a rock star," she muttered.

"Funny girl." I snickered in spite of myself. The red dimmed to pink.

"Just help me up." She reached out a hand, and let me haul her to her feet, but she wavered unsteadily.

Another rock came whistling over our heads. I saw a rustle in the woods. I ran at it full speed and tackled the body hiding in the bushes.

"Oof!" he exclaimed as he fell to the ground.

I raised my fist above his head. "Talk! Did Tom put you up to this?"

He laughed. It was Mark. He was in grade eleven. He should have more common sense than this kind of thing. "You wouldn't dare. You'll end up in jail." He spit up at my face.

I wiped off the spittle with the back of my sleeve. "Maybe I don't care whether I go to jail? Did you ever think of that? Maybe my sister is more important than where I live?"

"If you go to jail, who's going to look after her, idiot? You can't touch us. We're not stupid."

Sara came up beside us. She stepped on his chest. "Kieran might not be able to hurt you, but no one says I can't. I'm twelve. They can't arrest me. Just how badly did you want to hurt my brother? Because Mark, you loser, it's all coming back at you. Ready?"

Mark was staring up at her with stunned eyes, wriggling. She wound up and kicked him hard into the ribs.

It sounded like she'd dropped books onto her bed. "Is that all you've got?" He raised a rock, lining up to smash it down on me.

Sara wound up and powered her kick into his elbow. He howled as his arm changed alignment. The rock fell from his hand, smashing down on his own head. He howled again. 'You're going to regret that!" he yelled as he scrambled to his feet and headed down the road towards his house cradling his arm.

"Let's go, Kieran."

"He's going to say I did that."

She shrugged. "You and I both know the truth, and we'll make sure they know it. He was stalking us, remember? We just defended ourselves from him. He can't do anything."

"We should go home." I didn't like this. It felt wrong.

She shook her head. "We can't let them take our freedom. We're going to Maggie's, just like we planned." She grabbed my arm, and dragged me, until I stopped straining in the opposite direction. "I don't think we should, Sara. I don't like that lump on the back of your head."

She just shook her head, "I'm fine. I've had worse riding on my skateboard." She kept walking.

So, we went for ice cream. I kept looking behind me. Someone was going to be in trouble tonight. Sara bought me a rum raisin milkshake and picked up a double chocolate shake for herself. We sucked on the straws while we sat at the front window. I was scanning for whoever else was with Mark. I was sure that he hadn't been alone.

Sara licked a dollop of ice cream off her top lip and observed, "They're the losers, you know, not you."

I blinked at her over my cup. "What makes you say that?"

"It's obvious. You're looking after your little sister. That makes you the hero. You're protecting the helpless and the innocent." She batted her eyelashes at me in her best cute and innocent expression. "Obviously, you're the knight in shining armour, and he's the evil monster."

I loved her at that moment. Affection swelled up from my belly and lodged in my throat. She made me feel like I could do anything. No one was going to hurt my mom or my little sister. I didn't care if I ended up jail for it; I was going to protect them. I blinked back tears.

Sara drew the last of her shake up the straw with a rumble. "Mom's going to be home any time. We'd better get back and get dinner started, or she's going to rant at us."

I nodded. "Yeah. Let's go." I was on red alert as we walked, waiting for another rock to come flying, or someone else to start whispering in the bushes. My heart was pounding in my throat the whole way. We passed old Mrs. Weber and she scowled at me, but she didn't say anything. She wasn't the one whispering threats in the trees. If she was, this would be some creepy Sunday night movie.

We were in our drive way when they appeared. Tom, Mark, and three other guys. Jacob from grade eight was the youngest, the other two I didn't know. They were grade twelves. I'd seen them around, of course, because Laketon is little. "Sorry, guys." I said, sweeping Sara behind me with my left arm. "We're not interested in your party. We have things to do."

"Yeah, and you'll be doing them here on the front lawn."

"Are you stupid?" Sara mocked, "Someone is going to see you, and you'll be the ones arrested." One of the grade twelves grabbed her arm, and she thrashed around, trying to kick him.

"No one home at the moment." Tom said in that hoarse crackle that was the result of my punch. "Just us and you." He looked from me to Sara. "Who shall I pound first? You or that puny sister of yours?"

The other grade twelve grabbed Sara's other shoulder and pushed her toward Tom.

Tom grabbed her, and she lashed out, kicking wildly, bicycling her legs until she hit flesh. She raised a knee and the guy on her right side crumpled, groaning, and grabbing at his groin. The other one leaned in with a purposeful sneer on his face.

I exploded. Everything turned scarlet and I started swinging. While my body fought, my brain seemed to float up to the roof. I was watching everything happening below me.

Sara was screaming and lashing her body around, legs flying. Tom was on the ground again. I was flailing my arms around trying to hit anything that came near. Mom was in the drive way, adding her screams to Sara's.

Constable Hamilton and Corporal Fraser pulled up, sirens wailing.

Constable Hamilton pulled Tom off of me.

Corporal Fraser pulled the jerk off of Sara. "Making it a family affair, I see?" Corporal Fraser said, curtly. "I understand you are responsible for the broken arm over on Maple Street."

"Kieran didn't have anything to do with a broken arm." Sara shouted. "If you mean Mark, he was throwing rocks at us. Big ones! He hit us. We can show you the bruises. Look at this lump!" She pointed to the back of her head.

Constable Hamilton narrowed her eyes at me. "You didn't break his arm?"

I shook my head. "He was stalking us, like the rest of these guys. I just kept him from hurting Sara. I didn't touch anyone." The other guys were not looking nearly as sure of themselves now. They all glowered like they were hoods, but they knew they were in trouble.

"Sara?" Constable Hamilton said, "Is this true?"

"Kieran tried to stop Mark from hurting me. I was being attacked. I fought back when he tried to beat Kieran with a rock, and I broke the arm that had the rock before he could hurt him."

Too late I remembered lawyer John Malcolm's advice: "Don't make any statements."

My Mom was crying, shaking her fingers at Tom and his friends. "Why are you doing this to my kids? What did they ever do to you?"

Tom stared sullenly back at her, without saying anything.

"Come on," Constable Hamilton said to Tom, "get up." She reached onto her belt and unclipped her hand cuffs. Tom grinned at me, then his face changed as she snapped them around his wrists.

"Hey!" he squawked. "What are you doing that for! Kieran is the one on probation!"

"Tom King, I hereby charge you with assault of Sara Smith. You'll need to get into the back seat of the car. Watch your head."

I grinned over at Sara.

She looked at the others standing with Corporal Fraser. "Are you next? Every one of you tried to hurt us tonight!"

None of them would meet her eyes.

Once Tom was settled into the back seat of her squad car, Constable Hamilton strolled back over to us. "I'm calling Rob Sky. You're in breech of your probation."

"But…"

"It has to be filed. He'll record the reasonable grounds for the breech, and that you didn't intentionally set out to do so. It will probably be okay, but I'm still going to have to report it. Do you understand?"

I nodded.

"Have you had an appointment with the anger management clinician yet?"

"No.

My mom came and stood beside me. "He has one scheduled for tomorrow."

Corporal Fraser snickered. "That's ironic. Too bad it wasn't today, we might have avoided some unpleasantness. And Mark might not be at the hospital getting a cast put on his arm at this moment."

I shook my head. "Sara and I didn't do anything. We were minding our own business when they attacked us. That's the way those guys work. They've been following me, taunting me or threatening me all week. One of them has been making crank calls. They've been trying to make me crack and breech my order."

"But you didn't do it."

"I didn't." Until now. When I blew it, I did it thoroughly.

My mom put an arm around me and squeezed my shoulders. "I'm proud of you, Kieran."

"I know."

Mom glanced over to Sara. "I can't say I'm not a little worried about my sweet little girl, who apparently can break the arms of guys twice her size."

Sara smirked. "Doesn't it make you feel a little more confident of my safety? Obviously, I can look after myself."

I shook my head. "You're still my little sister. You're only twelve. You're not as tough as you think you are. You were lucky this time. Next time, they might beat the crap out of you."

"There isn't going to be a next time," Constable Hamilton interjected. "I'm not going to hear about either one of you beating up anyone, do you hear?"

"Yes, ma'am," Sara and I said in chorus.

Mom and Constable Hamilton exchanged looks. "Good," they said together.

~ Epilogue ~

I rode my dirt bike to the viewpoint and looked out at the lake and the winding streets of Laketon arrayed before me.

The scent of the pine trees made me breathe deeply, inhaling the fresh spring air with that special pungency that seemed to scrub negativity from my head.

Grade nine was nearly over.

Now that Tom was also on probation, things were much easier. He couldn't risk breeching his own order, so he left me alone.

We glared at each other in the halls at first, but little by little the animosity wore off, and now we just ignored each other. We were moving to what Mrs. Sykes called "cordial sufferance."

Everyone else mellowed out, too. I mean, what are you going to do? We all live in Laketon, and it's too small to have enemies. You can't avoid anyone well enough for that, as we learned the hard way.

Mrs. Sykes kept her eyes on me. Rob Sky asked me good questions, and he listened to my responses. He didn't judge my answers. He heard me. He connected me with some counsellors. They listened to me. They had some ideas about how to keep control of my temper. I practised them. Some days the strategies worked. Some days I lost it, but I didn't beat anyone up. It got easier, to stay in control.

Sara didn't have anyone threatening to beat her up. People knew she broke Mark's arm defending herself. No one else wanted a broken arm.

Mom kept loving us.

Dad didn't come visit.

I smiled as I watched a sailboat slicing through the water far below.

Everything was good in my world.

For now, at least.

Acknowledgements:

Thanks to Youth Probation Officer John who explained the youth justice procedures and process in BC, and generously offered his expertise by reviewing the manuscript to make sure I got it right.

Thanks also to Ty and Caryn for checking over the dirt bike scene.

Any mistakes are my own.

Life in Laketon 2

AFTER # 8

~ 1 ~

My hand hovered above the back doorknob. Sara was talking to someone in the kitchen. I strained to hear. Big brothers are expected to eavesdrop, after all. I couldn't make out what she was saying, so I turned the knob slowly and stepped inside.

"Ryan, listen to me!" My sister was shouting into the phone. She hadn't heard me come into the house. "No, this isn't about your girlfriend, of course I mean your OTHER girlfriend! I'm pregnant Ryan, do you hear me? You got me pregnant!"

I hesitated in the mud room. I doubted that this was news she meant for me to hear.

I could hear the buzzing of his voice on the other end of the line from out here.

I guess I could have backed up to give her some privacy, but it was cold outside, and besides, I was pretty sure I'd heard the worst already, so I stepped forward into the kitchen.

Her face screwed up at something he was saying, "I don't *know* what I'm going to do, that's why I'm calling you! I wanted to talk to you about what you thought we should do about *our* baby!"

More buzzing. The hockey playing scumbag who wore number eight was obviously not taking the news well at all.

Her anger changed suddenly as she gasped. She crumpled to

the floor, her eyes brimming with tears. "Ryan!" she whispered desperately, then the phone dropped onto her lap and she just cried. Occasionally she sputtered out, "Ryan" in a choked whisper and the tears gushed again.

I watched her for awhile, a tight little ball rocking on the floor. I knew I shouldn't say anything, but I couldn't help myself. "Did you think your darling Number Eight was going come back and marry you?"

"Screw you, Kieran."

"He's a hockey player, Sara. Hadn't you noticed they don't allow anything to get between them and their dreams of athletic glory? All you were ever going to be was a pleasant distraction. Such a shame you got caught."

The phone came whistling toward my head. I ducked just in time and it smashed into the wall. The back split off and the batteries spilled across the floor. I sighed and observed, "Mom is going to be really ticked off if you've broken the phone."

Sara stood up and stared hard at me.

I scowled back, "I suppose you could distract her from the broken phone by telling her you're pregnant. She probably wouldn't care at all about the phone after that news."

"You're a creep."

"Yeah, maybe, but you're the slut who got herself pregnant." I couldn't believe the words had come out of my mouth. I sounded like my father. Ah, crap. I sounded like our father.

Before I could apologize, she was on me. She jumped and then we were on the ground and she was pummeling me with her fists while she spattered me with her tears. "Take that back!" she cursed at me. "You take that back!"

She was just a kid, and I could have taken her, but I deserved the attack, and man, you don't hit a girl, especially not a pregnant girl. That was just sick. So I just lay on my back on the floor, my hands cupping her shoulders to push her a bit so that there was no force in her punches. I let her wear herself out while her tears rained down, drenching my shirt.

Finally her head sagged and she dropped her closed fists on my chest. She was heaving. I sat up, wrapping my arms around her, I whispered, "I'm sorry, Sara. I take it back." My own eyes were starting to sting a bit.

"I'm not a slut," she whispered.

"I know."

"He was the first."

"I kind of figured that." Man, she was only fourteen. I hope he was the first.

"You know what he said? Just now?" She sniffed. "He said 'how did I know the brat was his because it could have been anybody's.'" She shook her head and sputtered into my armpit. "It couldn't be anybody else's. There never has been anybody else."

"I'm sorry, Sara." I said again. I really meant it. This whole situation was just crap.

"I didn't exactly think we were going to be together forever or anything, but I thought he cared a *bit* at least. I thought he *liked* me." She sniffed again and snuggled into my chest. "I didn't even care that he had a girlfriend in Vancouver he's been with for two years already. I knew he wasn't going to pick me over her, but I thought he would be nice, at least."

My shirt was totally soaked now. I patted her on the back like she was five again and had just fallen off her bike. I used to do that a lot. It was my assigned job as her big brother.

Eventually she pulled back, wiped her eyes, and looked over at the bits of the phone scattered around us. "Help me pick these up. Maybe we can fix it before Mom gets home."

I leaned down and picked up one of the batteries. "Are you going to tell her?"

"Hell, no."

"She's going to figure it out eventually, you know, like when you're roughly the circumference of a whale."

Sara grimaced and looked away for a moment before she turned back and stared me down. "Maybe it won't get that far."

I met her eyes and translated the message she was sending me. "Oh."

"Don't tell her, okay?"

"She should know, Sara."

"Yeah, and she will, but just let me figure things out, okay? I want to have a plan when I tell her."

I nodded.

She leaned over and gave me a quick hug. "I forgive you for being a jerk."

"I forgive you for being pregnant." I said the words, because I knew I had to, but I didn't really mean it. I wouldn't forgive her for this one for a long time, if I ever did.

She snorted, and handed me the parts of the phone. "Better get to work. I have homework, and I am pretty sure you must, too."

I didn't have homework, of course. Even if the teachers assigned it, I didn't believe in homework.

~ 2 ~

As Sara shut her bedroom door, a slow anger burned through me.

My stupid sister is pregnant. I stared at the bits of phone, automatically sorting. Fourteen years old and pregnant. Rage overwhelmed me. How stupid could one person be? I worked the pieces of the phone into place. Didn't she know about birth control? How could she do this to Mom? How could she do this to us? I snapped in the batteries. If Sara had a baby, we were going to need more income. I was going to be stuck here in this stupid little tourist town forever doing menial jobs. I snapped the backing onto the phone and set it into the charger.

I couldn't stand to be in the house with her another minute. I was not going to be a calm big brother. I was supposed to graduate next year. I was supposed to get out. How could she ruin my life like this?

I slammed the back door and stumbled over to my dirt bike, thankful that I'd filled it with gas after my last ride. I revved the motor and raced up the road toward the hills.

This bike was salvation for me. When I was on my bike, the roar of the motor drowned out voices in my head: My mom's voice, so tired and sincere, asking me to sacrifice the money I was saving for an X Box so Sara could take dance lessons with her friends; Sara's voice, asking me to walk her to school instead of following that cute new girl, because Sara was scared of bullies; Ms. Sykes' voice, reminding me that I wanted to graduate; Dad's voice, the worst voice of all, shouting at mom that she was a lazy whore because she had asked him to help with grocery money.

Racing along the winding forestry roads above the lake I was free from everything. None of the troubles mattered any more.

Who cared about my dead beat father who didn't remember to send mom her cheques half the time?

Who cared about my grades?

Who cared about the wrinkles in Mom's forehead when she tried to stretch the money for rent, groceries, and then to try to get us stuff that other kids had?

Who cared about perfect Sara with the perfect grades, perfect friends, and perfect boyfriend? Surprise Mom. Sara is not so perfect after all.

I rode to the top of my favourite ridge and stopped the motor. Sometimes there were eagles up here, and once a deer had come out of the trees while I sat leaning against my bike. Sometimes I did that. I just sat. Out here nobody asked me whether I had homework to do, or whether I had some new computer game that we couldn't afford. Here I was free just to be alone and silent. Here nobody bothered me.

Here I was usually free from my thoughts.

Not today.

Today my thoughts had followed me: Stupid Sara! Her hot shot hockey player boyfriend had gone back to Vancouver when the team missed the play offs, so she was on her own.

The girls were idiots about the hockey players. They fell all over themselves to date one, even though everyone knew that most of them already had girlfriends in their home towns. They only came here to play for the season. Play hockey. Play girls. It wasn't a surprise when some girl ended up pregnant at the end of the season, but why did it have to be *my* sister this time?

We had enough trouble without a baby in the house. Mom was so tired all the time. Working days at the dairy and the occasional evenings at the pub hardly paid the bills. Where was the extra going to come from to get baby stuff?

My hands tightened into fists on the handles as I imagined beating stupid Number Eight into a bloody pulp. Even as I pictured it, I knew it wouldn't help, but it did make me feel a little better to imagine him lying crumpled on the grass.

What was Sara going to do? I had seen the fear in her eyes. Was Number Eight going to be "father of the year" like our dad was?

I thought about the last time our dad had come for a visit. He'd driven up in that old beaten up pick up and acted like he was happy to see us for about ten minutes, and then he looked bored. He asked me where he could get some weed. I mean really. I'm a kid, and he wants me to help him get drugs. Any loser in town could have helped him out with that, but I wasn't that much of a loser, and I sure wasn't going to help him do anything, especially not something that was going to end up hurting mom. Jerk.

He didn't stick around for long. He wrote Mom a cheque for a few months of late child support and pulled out one morning saying "something had come up" back in Alberta. Yeah right. Of course, the cheque had bounced. I was glad when he went. He wasn't a good dad when he was around, and I was a worse son. It made Mom stress when I was rude, and I couldn't help but be rude, because he made me so mad, coming and trying to pretend to be a family. It made me sick.

It was a miracle that he hadn't taken off when he got Mom

pregnant, come to think about it. He'd actually stuck around until Sara was three. Then he'd left to go work up north in Alberta and that was the end of that. I wished I'd had a dad who gave presents, came home every night, was nice to us, and actually paid the bills. It would have been great for Mom not to have all that worry and two kids as well. I was never going to be a father like him.

I sighed. No way around it. Life sucked if you were us. At least my dad had stuck around five years; that was five years longer than Number Eight was going to be around.

Suddenly I heard a noise off to edge of the trees. A soft, careful tread in the leaves once, then twice. Ever so cautiously, a doe came out from the trees. She didn't see me, and the wind was blowing my scent away from her. Her eyes were huge. I froze and watched her. She started eating. I watched her in the silence of the forest, letting the tranquility of the moment fill me. Time stretched.

The wind changed and the doe looked up. She stared at me, then turned and bounded back into the cover of the trees.

Wow.

I got back on my bike. When I fired it up, it sputtered like a machine gun, and I regretted the terror I knew would be causing in the woods. I felt less angry. I still thought Sara was an idiot, but I was starting to feel sorry for her, too. She was going to be lonely without Number Eight, even if he was a jerk. It was going to suck to blow up like a basketball, too. But she was going to have to take care of herself. No smoking and no drinking either, because there was no way she was going to have some damaged baby because she had no self-control and thought she should still be allowed to party. I was going to watch out for this little kid. Someone had to, because obviously my sister had no brains at all.

~ 3 ~

Sara and I didn't usually walk together, but today she had lagged behind until I left, instead of going early like she usually did. She liked to hang out in the cafeteria before school and catch up on all the latest news, since she didn't have a cell phone. Everyone else kept up through text messages. I walked a few steps ahead of her, wishing I'd been an only child.

"Hi, Sara!"

I looked up curiously at the tone in Kari's voice. Why did she sound so friendly? She hated Sara, but right now she was smiling with a happiness that only comes from having a delightful secret. I nudged Sara as we walked into the school. "She knows."

Sara shook her head. "No." That wasn't certainty in her voice. It was desperate hope. She headed off to her locker down the grade nine hall way. "See you this afternoon."

I grabbed her arm and leaned in to whisper, "She knows, Sara, and if Kari knows, everyone knows."

"Shut up. She doesn't know."

"Wishful thinking."

She glared at me so I just shrugged my shoulders and watched her head down the hall where the grade nines had their lockers. Stupid sister. Didn't she know anything about her own sex? Kari was way too smug not to have something huge to hold over Sara's head, and the only thing she could possibly have was pretty obvious.

I watched people in the halls as she walked by them. The word was definitely out. There was some weird teen girl telepathy passing the news like wildfire. Maybe it wasn't telepathy. Maybe it was just text messaging.

I saw girls looking at her belly suspiciously; I saw guys looking at her with something else in their eyes.

I was slow getting ready for PE. There were just three of us left in the locker room. Chris Turlock, a wannabe athlete, smirked at me. "Man, I can hardly wait for the next party. Your sister is going to have a *great* time."

"Shut up, man," responded my friend Dave.

"Oh, yeah. Ryan didn't have anything compared to what I can show her." Chris gave a pelvic thrust that made me want to puke.

"Chris, you're talking about his sister. Nobody wants to hear that," interrupted Dave. He snapped a shirt at Chris to distract him, but Chris was fixated.

"Ah, Davie Boy! Don't tell me you don't want to go down on her, too. That sweet little butt of hers, swinging by, just asking for a little action. You know she'd be a good ride."

"She wouldn't give you a look, Chris, with all that oozing slime on your back. Besides, you didn't score all season." Dave knew the right buttons to push.

"I scored. Just not on the ice."

"You didn't score with Sara."

Chris grinned, "Not yet, but she's mine for the taking."

"Since when?"

"Since Ryan warmed her up for me. She'll take *anybody*

now."

I stepped up between them, fury flooding me. "Are you saying my sister is easy?"

Chris laughed, "She's so easy, she would do me in here with you watching if I called her."

There was an explosion somewhere at the back of my brain, and then I was floating up by the ceiling, watching my arm move in slow motion toward Chris's jaw.

His head blew back, and then Chris was lying across the change room bench, groaning.

"Whoa, man!" Dave hooted. "I didn't know you had *that* in you."

I stared at Chris from above. His nose was bleeding and the blood was running down into his hair.

"Kieran?" Dave said, his voice echoing like it came from far away. "Are you okay? What's wrong with you?"

It felt like I was swimming through a fog as I came back into myself. I muttered, "He was asking for it."

Dave nodded. "Yup." He took a deep breath and asked, "So is it true?"

"What?"

"Is she pregnant?"

I glanced over to Chris, who was still groaning. "Why do you think so?" I wasn't saying anything until Sara was saying it.

"Ryan, man. He called some guys bragging about it."

I shook my head. "What a prince, eh?"

Dave sighed. "I like Sara, you know? I was going to ask her to the dance, but now…"

"You can still ask her, Dave. Even if she is pregnant, you know it isn't contagious."

Dave just looked at me for a minute, and then looked down

at Chris, still draped across the bench. "Should we try to help him up?"

I studied the blood dripping down his nose, across the cheek, and off the tips of his hair. "Nah. Let's just go to class."

So we did. We left him dripping and joined the class warming up by running around the track, and did the two extra laps Sanders assigned us for taking too long to get outside.

I had almost forgotten what had happened when Chris staggered out from the change room awhile later.

"Mr. Sanders!" Matt called, "Chris is hurt!"

Everyone raced in to surround him, except Dave and me. We walked in slowly, and were still twenty feet away when the whole class turned to stare at us. I shrugged at Dave, and headed to the school doors.

"Where do you think you're going, young man?" Mr. Sanders hollered after me.

"To the office, sir. I figured that's where you'd want me?"

Sanders scowled, draping his arm around Chris's waist, supporting him as they walked toward me.

Office party. That'd be fun.

Half an hour later the first aid teacher was swabbing up the blood and they decided, unfortunately, that Chris would survive. I sat and watched while they called his parents. They want him to go to the hospital to see if he had a concussion. Good for me.

"Well?" Ms. Sykes, the principal, asked succinctly.

"Ma'am?" We were sitting in her little office. Chris had been taken to the hospital by his parents, and it was time for The Chat.

"What did he say to make you pop him?"

"I'm sorry?"

She rolled her eyes then, and leaned back in her chair. "Come on. He's always shooting off his mouth and getting popped. You just seemed to hit him harder than most. What did he say?"

I wasn't going to say anything, but she just waited. It seemed like an hour while she watched me expectantly while I mused that no one said 'popped' when they meant 'punched' anymore. Finally I gave up; she was still watching me and waiting for my reply.

I sighed, "He made a crack about my sister being easy."

"Because she's pregnant?"

Wow. That was fast. Ms. Sykes was a whole lot smarter than I expected.

"She hasn't told anyone, yet."

"It appears the father isn't quite so discreet."

I nodded.

She looked at me thoughtfully for a minute, then she said, "You know that I have to suspend you for fighting?"

"Yes, ma'am."

"If I get teachers to assign homework for you while you're off, will you do it?" She was smirking now. It was a very small school. She knew all of our tendencies.

I shrugged. "Maybe."

She chuckled. "Try to make the effort, kiddo. It'd be nice if you could graduate. You're a good kid. You deserve a good future."

I didn't know what to say, so I didn't say anything. Teachers didn't usually think that I was a 'good kid.' They thought I was a pain in the butt. They thought I was a troublemaker. They thought I was a loose cannon. Ms. Sykes made me nervous, expecting me to be something more than the others did.

"I'll call your mom to come get you."

"She's working."

She looked at me for a while, reading me like I was a book. I had the distinct feeling that she understood what she was reading a lot better than I usually did.

"I'm sending you home. You'll have to stay there until next week. I'll send your homework home with Sara. Do it, okay?"

I nodded as I stood to go, and then turned at her office door, "Ms. Sykes? Don't say anything to my Mom. About Sara, I mean. She hasn't told her yet."

"You know that she's going to hear from someone else if Sara doesn't tell her soon?"

I nodded.

"You need to do some thinking this week. You can't just punch every loud mouth who makes a rude comment."

"I know. Thank you, ma'am."

She patted my shoulder and I felt her watching me thoughtfully as I left the building.

~ 4 ~

Mom dropped her purse on the counter with a rather purposeful thud, and spun to stare at me as I sat casually at the kitchen table playing a Game Boy I'd found at the thrift store. She put her hands on her hips and shook her head. "Ms. Sykes called me at work."

"Yeah. I figured she would." I didn't look up.

"Are you trying to drive me to drink?"

I snorted. Dad drank. Sometimes he drank a lot. Mom never touched a drop. She said she didn't need to, because our dad drank enough for all of us. I'd seen enough of that that I didn't drink either. Sara drank. I was going to have to have a little chat with her about that.

Mom shook her head again and sighed. That made me feel worse than if she'd been screaming at me.

"She said you were in a fight."

"Well, not exactly a fight."

She tilted her head and raised an eyebrow. "Oh? How so?"

"It was just one punch. One punch isn't a fight."

Her eyes widened and she leaned over. She spoke very slowly, "Ms. Sykes said that the other boy had to go to the hospital. They were worried he had a concussion."

"Yeah. I figured."

SHAWN L. BIRD

"He didn't hit you first?" She sounded hopeful.

I stared at the game and shook my head.

"What on earth happened that you felt such an overwhelming urge to hit him? You haven't hit anyone since, well you know." Her voice trailed off.

Yeah. I knew. Back in grade nine I'd had some serious temper issues. I had put a kid in the hospital. I'd been charged with assault and had to see a counselor and probation officer. It was hard, but it was probably the best thing that ever happened to me, having all those people to talk to. They helped me get control of myself. It'd been two years since my brain had exploded and I'd lost it like that. I was a little freaked out about it, actually.

Mom was looking expectant. "Hon?"

I sighed, "He said something."

"What did he say?"

"He insulted someone. He deserved it, Mom."

"Hon, you know that violence is not the answer to something like that. You're lucky this time. Ms. Sykes says he is okay."

I grunted noncommittally at the news. "If you knew what he'd said, you would be glad I did it."

She scowled at me doubtfully.

I met her eyes as I assured her, "Trust me."

She pulled up her chair and sat down across from me. "Well, I guess at this point it doesn't really matter how it happened. You're suspended for the rest of the week. What do you plan to do with yourself?"

I shrugged. I planned to do as little as possible, but I wasn't going to tell her that.

"The dairy is hiring."

"Huh?"

She dropped an application form on the table in front of me.

"If you are not going to school, then you can go work somewhere that will bring us in a bit of money. Tonight I want to see your completed resumé and you're going to have this form filled out. Tomorrow you're going to drop them off at the dairy at seven a.m. and tell them you're ready to start immediately."

"Mom…"

"You're working. Is that clear?"

I sighed. "Yeah."

"Yeah what?"

"Yeah, it's clear. I don't think they'll hire me though."

She smirked. "Oh, they will. I've already spoken to Rick. Wear rubber boots."

~ 5 ~

That's how I ended up spending what would have been a pleasant break from school shoveling manure.

I suppose it wasn't much different from school. I felt like I was shoveling manure in the classroom, too, as I tried to pass by telling teachers what they wanted to hear, year after year.

Actually, the dairy was not a bad place to work. I drove the small tractor through the huge barn and pushed the manure out into the pile in the yard. When I was done that, I moved manure around the yard. Then I helped push feed down to the cows. The feed was carefully measured for each cow.

I helped sterilize the milking equipment that my Mom connected where she worked in the milking room. Just before it was time to go home, I helped get the cows moving through the milking room. My last task was sterilizing the equipment afterwards. It was a very regular routine, and there was something comforting about the warm placid cows chewing their cud and blowing foggy breaths in the cold air. It was physical and hypnotic. I forgot about my stupid sister for hours.

I even got used to the smell of the manure. I guess you can get used to any stink if you don't get out of it long enough to smell the air without it.

I also was able to hand my mother a decent pay cheque at the end of the week. She smiled when I handed it over.

"You need some spending money; how much of this would you like back?"

I shook my head. "Nothing. Keep it all."

She looked at me for a bit before she suggested, "Feeling guilty?"

I shrugged.

"Well, I won't say that we can't use all of it. This will come in handy."

"You have no idea," I muttered.

"What?"

I shook my head, as Sara came in on a wave of cold air.

"Hi, Mom." Her voice was funny.

Mom looked over at her and her eyes widened with alarm when she saw the expression on Sara's face. She rose from her chair and reached out, "Sara?"

"I need to talk to you, Mom." She glanced over to me.

Oh. Today was the day. No wonder she looked nervous.

I stood up to give her some privacy, but she put her hand on my shoulder. "You might as well stay."

True, if there was a witness Mom was probably less likely to kill her. On the other hand, maybe she'd want to kill both of us. As the big brother, I was supposed to keep Sara out of trouble.

Sara sat down next to me on the couch and inhaled deeply. "Mom, do you remember Ryan?"

Mom sucked in her breath. I was pretty sure that she guessed the news right then.

Sara continued, "Before he left, we…well, um." She stared hard at the floor before glancing up at me. I gave her hand a squeeze and she took a deep breath. She looked up at Mom, "I'm pregnant."

My mom just looked at her for a long time. Finally she said in a hushed voice, "I'd kind of hoped you'd have a little longer childhood than this."

No anger, just sadness.

Sara stood and enveloped Mom in a hug. "I'm so sorry, Mom. I'm so sorry."

Mom hugged her, rocking her back and forth, and suddenly I saw Sara when she was four being rocked just that way after a visit from our dad.

Mom pulled back, and pushed the hair out of Sara's eyes, "Have you told Ryan?"

Sara nodded.

"How did he take the news?"

Sara just shook her head and nestled more tightly into Mom's embrace. Mom looked over her shoulder at me with her eyebrows raised.

"He's a jerk, too."

"And the boy at school? The one you punched?"

I nodded, "Another jerk."

"I see," she said. She really did.

~ 6 ~

Mom was getting out the snow shovel when I got home. She looked tired.

"I'll take that," I said, reaching to take it out of her hand. "You go in and put your feet up."

Her eyebrows went up. "Are you trying to butter me up?" She studied me suspiciously. "Did you get into trouble at school again?"

I laughed. "No, I'm great. I'll shovel."

She sighed. "You're a good kid."

"I've been telling you that for years."

She nodded, "I know this has been rough on you. I mean the divorce. Your dad. Now this with Sara."

"It's okay, Mom."

"No, listen. I wish I could have given you more. You deserve more opportunities than I have been able to give you. I'm sorry about that."

"Mom."

"I appreciate all you do around here. I just want you to know that. You are a great son, even if you're not the greatest student," she reached out and ruffled my hair. I leaned away laughing as she continued, "I am thankful that Sara has got such a caring big brother to support her right now." She patted me on the back and then pulled me in for a hug. "I love you," she whispered. Her breath warmed my cold ear.

"Love you too, Mom." I blinked a few times. The cold was making my eyes burn. "I should get to work before I freeze out here."

"Oh, right." She smiled at me gently. "I'll get dinner started." She went inside while I cleared the driveway.

It wasn't a big driveway, but the steady rhythm of scraping of the shovel on the ground and tossing off the load of snow felt good. Thinking about Sara's baby stressed me out. I went fast, and my muscles were aching when Sara came up the road.

She was crying again. Frozen lines tracked down her cheeks. "You okay?"

She shook her head.

"What happened?"

She shook her head again, as if she was going to shake out the memory of whatever it was.

"Sara, come on. What is it?"

She sniffled and whispered, "I don't know what to do."

We walked down the driveway and I put the shovel away.

She leaned against the wall. "There was a fight. Kari was saying how it was no big deal to have an abortion, and Ricky was freaking out and saying that it was murder. Kari said only idiots have babies when they're teens. Ricky said only murderers kill babies. Then they both tried to get me to tell them what I was going to do. My choices were to be a murderer or an idiot."

"Oh, Sara." I held out my arms and she leaned in, weeping quietly on my shoulder.

Poor kid. What were we going to do?

Sara and I were walking to school on Monday when Ricky

called out, "Hey Sara! You decided yet whether you're a murderer?"

She flashed him a glare.

I stared at him until he met my eyes.

"You a murderer too?" he challenged.

"Lay off my sister, Ricky. She doesn't need your crap."

"What are you going to do about it?"

Ricky was not the brightest kid in school, but you'd think he'd know better than to pick a fight with the kid who was barely off a suspension for beating someone. "I'd rather not do anything about it, but I will if I have to."

"Bring it on wimp. Your sister deserves whatever she gets."

My brain flashed and I fought to keep myself in my head, and to keep my fist at my hip.

"Scared?" he hissed with a challenge.

I narrowed my eyes, and saw my arm take the punch. I saw him bleeding on the ground, like Chris had lain a month earlier. It would be so satisfying, and so fast. It'd be so easy. He thought he was tough, but he wasn't fast enough to block me, and one connecting punch is all it would take.

I smiled in what I hoped was a terrifying way and turned my back on him. I could feel tremors starting from the adrenaline that was rushing through my system. I walked into the school, breathing deeply, trying to think calm thoughts.

"Scaredy-cat!" he called after me, but I think there was a little relief in his voice. If he'd really wanted to fight, he would have run after me.

I opened the office door and sat down on the cracked vinyl bench, thinking how absurd it was to call someone 'scaredy-cat.' I put my head on my knees and tried not to shake too badly. The vision of his bloody face was clear in my head, and I was battling myself not to go back out and make it reality.

A gentle hand touched my shoulder, "Hey."

Ms. Sykes.

"You okay?" she whispered.

I shook my head without looking up.

She tapped my shoulder again and said, "Come into my office."

I stood and followed her, sitting down without meeting her eyes.

"You wanted to punch someone?" she said frankly.

I nodded.

"But you didn't."

I shook my head.

"Good for you. Stay in here a little while and recover yourself in some privacy. If you need to talk about it, you can find me. Okay?"

I nodded.

"I'm proud of you. It must have been hard to walk away."

I nodded again as she shut the door behind her.

My head was churning and it was ages before the shaking stopped. When the bell rang, I rose and headed out of the office. Ms. Sykes was standing talking to a kid. She looked up as I came past and met my eyes. She tilted her head just slightly.

I nodded in response. Yes. I'd be okay.

~ 7 ~

A loud roaring woke me out of a sound sleep. For a moment I whipped my head back and forth, afraid that the house was falling down, but then I realized the sound was coming from the bathroom. Something was dying in there, and whatever it was, it was not happy about it. Another roar drew me cautiously out of bed, and I tiptoed across the hall. Mom's bedroom door was closed. Sara's was open.

I tapped gently on the bathroom door. "Sara? Are you okay?"

Another roar.

"Sara?"

"Go away." It was the wimpiest voice you've ever heard.

The water ran for a few moments, and then I heard the unmistakable sounds of tooth brushing, gargling and the rest of those sounds you expect to hear in a bathroom. I slid down the wall to sit on the floor and wait for her.

The door opened a crack and she stuck her head out. "Go back to bed."

"I don't think so. You sound like you're dying." She didn't look very good, either. Her hair was sticking to the sweat beads on her forehead and her eyes had black circles under them.

"Do you think you have the flu?"

She rolled her eyes at me.

"What?"

She pointed to her belly. "Pregnant. Idiot."

"So?"

"So I've got morning sickness. Obviously."

"But it's the middle of the night!"

"Oh, God, you're stupid," she growled as she staggered back to her bedroom.

Whatever you've heard about the joyful blossoming of pregnancy, throw it out the window. I discovered pretty quickly that all the stuff I had heard was wrong. Take morning sickness for example. First of all, it doesn't just happen in the morning. It happens all day long, and all night long as well. Apparently some people never vomit once in their entire pregnancy. Not Sara. Sara was a vomit factory.

She would be walking home from school with me, chatting about something and then her face would change to a pasty shade of green and she'd be racing for a bathroom. Occasionally she wouldn't make it, and the resulting mess was way more than I wanted to be involved in my sister's pregnancy, let me tell you.

I'd see her sprinting down the halls at school, lips pressed so tightly together than she looked like she'd been sucking on lemons. One day I was sitting in the office and Jan Hollidale came in cursing with her hands over her face.

Mrs. Parker, the secretary, hushed her and got her an ice pack. "What happened, dear?" she asked gently.

"That girl is a menace!" Jan snarled. "She rammed the door right into my face! I think she broke my nose!"

I wondered who was showing such violent tendencies when Sara came into the office, brows furrowed. "Sorry, Jan."

Jan grunted and turned away.

"Can I help somehow?" Sara pleaded.

"You can help by letting someone know you're coming before you slam through the door!"

I snickered and Jan glared at me. "Not a good idea, actually. Trust me. It's much better if she keeps her mouth shut." I knew that asking Sara to open her mouth at the bathroom door was asking for a shower in toxic waste.

Jan looked at me for a moment before her eyes widened and her nose curled.

After that day, someone was assigned to run ahead of Sara and call warnings at the class room doors. My math class cracked up the first time we heard the shout of "Step away from the door! Barfing girl coming through!" as Sara tore past.

"You wouldn't believe it, Mom. It's hilarious." I told her one evening at dinner.

Sara glared. "Thanks for being so considerate."

"It's funny, Sara."

"It is *not* funny, jerk. I feel like a leper that's calling, 'Unclean! Unclean!' It's embarrassing."

"If you don't do it, someone else will be the one who is unclean. Isn't that the point?"

She punched me in the arm. That girl has a heavy duty right hook for someone who weighs about a hundred pounds. I rubbed my arm and laughed at her as I started clearing the dishes.

Mom just shook her head.

~ 8 ~

Sara was standing by her locker shaking.

"Hey."

She swallowed, but didn't say anything.

"You want to go?"

She nodded, and I helped her gather her stuff.

"Mr. Jones? Sara? Where are you going?" Ms. Sykes was watching from the office door.

I couldn't very well tell her we were going to skip, could I?

"Would you two like to talk in the counseling room?"

I nodded.

As Sara collapsed onto the ratty couch, I asked, "What's wrong?"

She shook her head.

"Sara, tell me."

She sniffed and looked away.

I didn't ask again. We just sat side by side. When I glanced over at her a few minutes later, tears were dripping down her cheeks. "It might help to talk about it, you know."

She swallowed loudly, and then muttered. "It isn't right."

"What?"

"You know how Kari's mom breeds purebred dogs?"

I nodded.

"Apparently some neighbourhood dog got into their yard, and got their show bitch pregnant."

"Ah."

"So Kari was telling me about how they took it in to the vet and aborted the puppies. She said there were seven." She sniffed again. "Seven dead puppies."

I considered pointing out they were just puppies, but I figured she'd hit me, so I waited for the rest of the story.

Suddenly she burst into tears as she collapsed howled, "I don't want to kill my baby!"

I sat down beside her, "Who says you should?"

Her howls just got louder. I rubbed her back absently. "Do you think it would hurt to have an abortion?"

"Hurt me? Or hurt the baby?"

What kind of stupid question was that? Obviously it was going to hurt the baby. Killing was kind of the point, after all. I guess that answered my question.

She pushed her head back and stared at the ceiling. "I don't want to have the baby, either though. I don't want to be huge or to push a watermelon out of me!"

I shrugged. "Not too many other options besides having the baby or aborting it."

She put her arm across her eyes and sighed, "Man, my life sucks."

The bell rang. "Do you want to sit in here? I have to go to class."

She nodded, and I slipped out the door.

"Mr. Jones?"

I turned to see Ms. Sykes standing behind me. "Yes, ma'am?"

"Can I see you in my office, please?"

I nodded and followed her down the hall. She shut the door behind her and indicated a chair.

"I'm concerned about your sister."

"Yeah. Me, too."

She wrinkled her brow. "I don't wish to pry, but I'm quite alarmed by the changes I've noticed."

I nodded.

"How is she at home? Does she have someone to talk to about things?"

I shrugged. "Yeah, I guess."

Ms. Sykes shook her head. "She is refusing to talk to Mrs. Dunn."

"Yeah." Mrs. Dunn was an ancient guidance counselor. Sara called her 'Mrs. Dumb' at home and muttered about people needing to mind their own business.

"It's really important that Sara has someone to help support her. This is a rather challenging time for her and I'm quite concerned to see her grades being impacted."

So that was it. Sara herself wasn't the issue. Losing Sara's straight A average was going to pull down the school's averages. "I don't think she's feeling well enough to be doing homework all evening any more."

Ms. Sykes nodded. "I know she's been quite sick with her pregnancy. She's through the first trimester now though. Usually things improve in the second trimester."

I shrugged again. I wasn't an expert in pregnancy.

She patted me on the back, "Thanks for your time. Make sure Sara knows that we're here to help with whatever she needs."

"Thanks, Ms. Sykes." Personally, I think what Sara needed was a boyfriend who wasn't a jerk, a father who paid child support, a mom who didn't have to work all the time, and a brother who was smart enough to do well in school and big enough to beat up lecherous hockey players who thought it was fun to have sex with fourteen year olds. But that was just me.

Mom set the dinner plates on the table and said, "What's up?" as she caught sight of Sara's red eyes.

"I'm only fourteen. I'm too young to be making life and death decisions!" Sara sputtered.

Mom inclined her head. "I would agree with you, except here you are. When you made the choice to enter a sexual relationship with Ryan, you were accepting this responsibility. Part of being mature enough for sex is recognizing there are consequences involved."

Sara blushed. "There wasn't much *thinking* about anything at the time."

Mom nodded. "I know. I'm not sure I gave any of this much thought when I had sex the first time either, but that doesn't mean it isn't true. Our actions have consequences. If you have sex, you may get pregnant. It's pretty basic."

"Well, we know I did. So now what should I do?" Sara pouted, setting her chin into her hands. She looked at me.

I raised my hands, "Don't look at me. I'm just the uncle." Never mind that I'd have to help the thing, and be kept up all night listening to its squawling.

Mom shook her head. "Sara, this is *your* body, *your* baby, *your* choice. I'm not going to tell you what to do, and you can't ask Kieran to, either. Any choice will be hard. You just have to pick your pain. I'm sorry, honey. No one else can make this decision for you."

"Can't you give me a hint?"

Mom smiled. "If you keep the baby, you'll be financially

stretched, you'll get no sleep for several months, your school work will suffer, and in fifteen years, you risk having this conversation with her. She will fill your life with stress, aggravation and worry, but she will also be your greatest joy and pride. You will wonder all the time, if you did the right thing, if you gave her the best chance, if you gave *yourself* the best chance."

Sara nodded. "Her? You think it's a girl? You think I shouldn't keep her?"

Mom shrugged her shoulders, "Her. Him. Whatever it is. If you abort the baby, you will have a few days of discomfort. You'll go back to school and life will probably seem much the same as before, but you will be changed by the experience. You will still know when your baby would have been born, and you'll always see children that age and wonder if you made the right decision. Only you will know what the true cost of that decision will be, and you won't know until after the operation."

Sara scowled. "Great."

Mom continued, "If you put your baby up for adoption, you'll wonder for years where she is. You'll wonder about her parents. You'll wonder how she's doing and if she's being treated well. You'll wonder if you did the right thing. The only constant between your choices is not knowing whether another choice could have been the better one. But Sara, you can't live your life worrying whether you were right or wrong. You can't doubt yourself. You have to make the best choice for who you are right now and accept the consequences." She took Sara's hand.

"No single choice is going to be right for everyone. My choice might not be your best choice, hon. I could never presume to tell you what you should do. You have to get all the information you can. You're a smart girl. You'll make the right choice for you."

"I'm beginning to doubt that there is a right choice."

I spoke up, "Maybe it's about not making the wrong choice, more than it's about making the right choice."

Mom laughed.

Sara groaned, "Thanks, Kieran. That's really helpful."

~ 9 ~

The next week, Sara was standing in the office when I went past on my way to PE. I paused and studied her. Her lips were tight and her eyes looked haunted.

I went in. "Hey."

She looked over at me with those strange sad eyes. "Yeah?"

"What are you doing in the office?"

"Signing out."

"Mom will be ticked off if you miss more school. Where are you going?"

She narrowed her eyes. "I have a doctor's appointment. Do you mind?"

"Does Mom know?"

"Of course she knows. She made the appointment. She's working, though. She can't take me. So I am walking."

I sighed, leaning close to whisper so the secretary couldn't hear me. "What's wrong?"

Her lips quivered slightly, and she pulled my arm to whisper into my ear in a shaky voice, "I'm scared."

"Do you want me to come with you?"

Her eyes flickered. "Will you?"

I nodded, "Yeah." I tilted my chin toward the gym. "It's not like it'll hurt me to miss running around the field for an hour."

A purposeful cough interrupted us. "Mr. Jones, what's this I'm hearing?"

"I'm going with Sara to her doctor's appointment." I said to the secretary.

She nodded, "Sounds like a good idea. She rifled through the file and passed me my attendance card. I signed, and Sara and I headed out the door.

"What are you scared about?" I asked as the door closed behind us. We were half way to the clinic before she answered.

"This is the appointment when I am supposed to tell him my decision."

"Decision?"

She looked straight ahead and her voice was flat. "Whether or not I terminate the pregnancy."

I swallowed. "Oh." Great. Lucky me. "What have you decided?"

She shrugged.

"You don't know, or you're not telling me?"

She sighed and shook her head. The clinic was just ahead. "I still don't know."

We walked up the steps and pushed through the door. The antiseptic miasma hit me and I glanced over to Sara. If I were prone to morning sickness, one whiff of that and I'd be in barf mode. She didn't seem to mind, though. She went straight to the counter, "Hi, Cynthia."

"Hi Sara, have a seat. Dr. Smith will be with you shortly." Cynthia looked up and noticed me. "Hello there. We haven't seen you in a while. How are you doing these days?"

"Fine, thanks." In a small town, everyone knows you, and Sara and I had been coming to this office since we were babies.

Sara picked up a ratty gossip magazine and flicked through

it aimlessly. She paused and stared at one page.

I sat down next to her and looked over to see what she was staring at. It was a spread about celebrity moms. Happy looking mothers cuddled adorable cherubs.

"They make it look so simple," she said. "Look at how beautifully they're dressed. Even the babies have expensive designer outfits."

"Very wasteful." I said, sagely.

She scowled. "That's not what I mean. Look at us," she said waving her hands to me. "We have barely enough. Mom struggles all the time just to get by. I'm just a kid. I'm not ready to be anybody's mother!"

"It's a huge responsibility." I agreed. "So does that mean you've decided…"

"No!" she snarled.

Cynthia looked up.

Sara took a deep breath and tried again, calmly. "No," she said. "I haven't decided anything. I can't raise a baby, but I don't think I can kill it either." A tear formed in her right eye and slowly travelled down her cheek. "I have no idea what to do."

Dr. Smith came into the waiting himself, "Hello, Sara." He noticed me beside her and added "Kieran, nice of you to bring your sister."

Sara stood up, swinging her back pack onto her shoulder. "Can he come in with me?"

I looked up sharply. "What? Why?"

She gave me one of those, 'Why are you so stupid?' looks that sisters are so good at.

I rolled my eyes.

Dr. Smith laughed. "Sure he can, if he wants to."

Sara gave me the 'you're coming in or I will hurt you' look.

"Fine." I said, standing. "I'll come."

I trailed after them self-consciously. Cynthia looked up as we went by, pinching her lips tightly to keep from smiling.

Sara climbed up onto the examining table. Dr. Smith took her blood pressure, her temperature, and her pulse, then Sara swung her feet up and leaned back, unzipping her jeans.

I looked away.

Dr. Smith took out a measuring tape and measured her belly. Then, as she zipped up again and sat up, he wrote in her chart.

I waited.

Sara shifted uneasily on the table.

Dr. Smith looked up. "So, have you made your decision?"

She shook her head. "Can I ask you a question?"

"Of course." He smiled at her to set her at ease.

"I read about how an abortion is done. They're safe if they're done in the hospital?"

He nodded, "Every medical procedure has some risks, but in a hospital with proper monitoring, yes. The procedure is quite safe."

"Would I have to stay over night in the hospital?"

"No, it's an outpatient service. You'd be discharged in a few hours."

"How long would I be away from school?"

"If you have the procedure Friday, you should be fine to attend on Monday. You just wouldn't be able to run around in PE for a couple of weeks."

She nodded thoughtfully. "I just have one more question."

"Ask away."

"If you tried, could you hear the baby's heart beat now?"

He didn't answer for a minute, and then said, "Why do you ask?"

She narrowed her eyes at him. "Because I don't want to miss any information that might impact my decision." She tightened her face into the 'I will win this' face. I could have told him to give in.

He must have had a sister himself, because he just nodded. "Yes, the heart beat is discernable at this stage."

"When did it start beating?"

"About four weeks after you conceived. You're at least ten weeks along. If you choose to terminate your pregnancy, you have only a couple of weeks when it can be done simply in one of the local hospitals. You understand that, right?"

Sara nodded. She looked at me.

"Refusing to decide is a decision, too." I said.

She looked at Dr. Smith. "I've decided."

He waited.

She took a deep breath. "I want to hear the heart beat."

"I'm not sure that's the best idea."

She narrowed her eyes again in that 'don't you even consider arguing with me' look and he sighed. He *definitely* had a little sister.

He put a little goop on her belly and then set a pen-like thing on it. Suddenly, through the room there echoed a fast "Whoosha-whoosha" sound.

Sara blinked and tightened her lips, inhaling deeply. Then she glanced at me and grinned.

She looked at Dr. Smith with the intensity of certainty. "I'm having the baby," she said with one emphatic nod, "but I don't know if I can raise it. I need you to get me information about adoption."

"Are you sure, Sara?" I said. "You want to go through all of that trouble and then give away the baby?"

"I'm sure I'm not killing it." She shrugged. "That's all I know."

"All right." Dr. Smith said. "In that case, talk to Cynthia on the way out and make an appointment for four weeks from now." Sara hopped off the examining table. "And pick up a good guide on what to expect when you're pregnant. It'll set your mind at ease. He opened the door and we stepped out. "Good luck, my dear."

Sara grinned up at him. All the tension had left her body when she made the decision. "Come on, Kieran. Let's go back to school."

I followed her out of the clinic feeling like my world had exploded. With her decision, she had doomed us all. She wasn't going to be able to give away her baby. Who could do that? I was going to have to stay here and be the responsible man around our house. I would have to quit school and get a job to help pay for Sara's baby. I loved my sister, but right now, I hated her.

She turned around, "What's wrong?"

"Nothing."

She wrinkled her brows and tilted her head, but we were already back to school.

"See you at home," I said.

~ 10 ~

Summer came. I was hired back at the dairy. Sara got on at Tim Hortons. She was worried about tourists' reactions to her, but the uniform was loose enough to hide her belly.

It was already twenty-five degrees at nine o'clock, and the forecast said it was heading to forty. Our house doesn't have air conditioning, and electric fans don't cut it when it's forty degrees. The house just goes from being an oven, to being a convection oven.

"Hey Sara, let's go to the beach before we work this afternoon."

She scowled at me.

"Oh, come on. Everyone already knows you're pregnant. Who cares?"

She got all teary then. Oh. I haven't mentioned that part of pregnancy yet, have I? Besides the all day every day sickness, there are mood swings: dramatic pin-ball action between as many emotions as possible within a day. Heck. Within an hour. Who am I kidding? She could go from laughter to fury to despair in practically the same minute. It was exhausting. I tried to be patient.

"Sara, get over yourself. Go put on your bathing suit and put a t-shirt on over the top of it if you're shy. No one will think anything of it."

"I feel like a whale."

"Seriously, it's hardly noticeable to anyone else. Just come. You'll boil if you stay inside today."

She grudgingly agreed to come and I waited for her, practicing my patience thing again. She took awhile, and made lots of funny, squeaky noises while she was in her room. I think she was crying. When she finally came out, t-shirt and shorts over her bathing suit, I could see that her eyes were red.

I tried to smile naturally and not show my irritation. "Ready to go?"

She sniffled. "I look like a whale, too."

"No, you don't. Seriously, I'm sure none of the tourists will notice anything."

As we walked I tried to tease her to get her smiling, but she wasn't being very cooperative. It was going to be a long day.

Thankfully, when we got to the beach, some of her friends from school had their towels all together and they shouted at her to join them. She looked at me, "Is it okay? You don't mind?"

I laughed. "No, go hang out with them. I'll find something to do." I'd seen a couple of cute tourist girls.

Sara looked at me suspiciously, so I wiggled my eyebrows suggestively at the intended prey. She followed my eyes and sighed, "Good *luck*."

I snickered at her doubt.

As she set out her towel she added, "Don't get anyone pregnant, eh? I don't think Mom could take it."

I laughed at that. There was no way I was getting myself tangled up in anyone else's pregnancy nightmare. I was spending too much time in my sister's.

I had been slow to recognize the benefits of living in a tourist town when it came to developing romantic technique. Some of my classmates were actively working the tourist girls before their voices had broken. I had mixed with them on the beach playing volleyball on the shore and tag in the waves, of course, but I had missed the fact that you can afford to make a lot of mistakes when you are not likely to see the girl again. That's kind of reassuring. Makes polishing your game quite easy. You get a new start every day.

I was flirting with a red headed girl from Edmonton who said her name was Chancey, when I noticed Sara talking to Kari. Well, Kari was talking. Sara was just staring at the lake with an agonized expression.

Chancey whacked me gently in the arm, "Hey you. Are you listening?" She shook her shoulders and the bounce at the front of her bikini snatched my attention back.

I tried to look at her face and focus on her words. She filled out her bikini well, so her words were hard to hear. I glanced back at Sara. Kari looked over at me and met my eyes as she talked.

"Hey." Chancey scowled, "You got a thing for that girl?"

"Huh?"

"That girl over there in that group. Are you trying to use me to get her jealous or something?"

"Which girl?"

She scoffed, "The one in the red bikini, obviously."

I shook my head. "Kari? Definitely not."

"Okay. Then the one in the Metallica t-shirt."

"No, that's my sister. She's going through some stuff. Kari is trouble. I'm just keeping an eye on her."

Chancey sighed. "Well, so much for my summer romance."

"What?"

She sighed dramatically, "Go to your sister, handsome. I'll find another distraction." She picked up her towel, shook out the sand so it stuck onto my wet legs, and headed off in the opposite direction, towards some guys playing volleyball.

I thought of chasing after her, but looked back at Sara. Kari and the others had gone into the water, but Sara was sitting on her towel, staring out at the lake. She didn't look like she was seeing it, though. I said good bye to my chance with Chancey, and dropped beside Sara.

"What happened?"

"Kari was talking about Dad."

"Dad is none of her business, don't worry about it."

"She says she saw him at the grocery store today."

"No way," I shook my head, swallowing a stab of dread. "He's in Alberta. He wouldn't come here."

At that moment, just to make a liar out of me, the loser himself showed up on the beach, wearing cut-offs and a cowboy hat. He'd pulled off his t-shirt and was holding it in his hand. His belly looked like a perogi. He hadn't shaved recently. I could see how red his eyes were from here.

"Oh, god," I groaned. "Turn around. Don't let him see us."

But good ol' dad had his radar working and he zeroed in on us. He got this big sappy grin on his face, and strolled over like we were his favourite thing in the world. "Kieran! Son! You look great!"

I grunted, and looked down the beach, where Chancey had joined the volley ball game.

He looked down at Sara. "I heard a rumour about you spreading your legs for a crappy right wing."

Sara inhaled and stared down at her towel. I think she was sucking in her stomach.

"Well, is it true? Are you a tramp like your mother?"

"That's rich, coming from you," I said, standing up and moving in front of him. "You're the one who left, remember?" I could smell beer on his breath. It wasn't even eleven o'clock in the morning yet.

Dad scowled, "I should have left when she got pregnant if I'd had any sense." He stared at Sara, "You're just like her, trying to trap a guy by the cock. Looks like the jock had more sense than me."

I hit him.

He dropped into the sand like a sack of rotten fruit, collapsing in on himself.

Sara stared at me, tears dripping down her face.

"Come on," I said. "I'm taking you for ice cream." The ice cream place had air conditioning, at least.

~ 11 ~

It was hot and humid in the barn where I stood watching the cows after the evening milking. I'd distracted myself from the events of the morning with hard work. They'd cut hay this morning, and I'd helped stack the bales. Now I just watched the cows, placidly chewing, and inhaled the strangely comforting scent of manure, fresh cut hay, and my own sweat.

"Your dad texted me," Mom said, coming up beside me.

"Bully for him." I walked out to the paddock fence, my back to her.

She sighed and followed me. "He's your father, Kieran. I know he's not perfect, but he's the only father you've got."

"You could marry a millionaire."

She laughed, "Yes, me and my designer footwear." She glanced down at her rubber boots, thick with muck, then looked out over the fields, past the cows in the paddock. "You hurt his feelings, you know."

"He doesn't have feelings."

"Kieran."

"He'd been drinking. I could smell it on his breath. He was insulting Sara."

She inhaled deeply. "He has issues. I know that, but he's your father. He wants to be part of your life. You need your dad,

Kieran. It doesn't hurt you to give him a chance."

I crossed my arms, snorting.

She put an arm around my shoulder. "I love how you're standing up for Sara. Let's go home." She tugged on my bicep and sauntered to the car. "You're getting more muscled."

I shrugged, but smirked to myself. Hauling bales at the dairy was better than weights any time.

She wrinkled her nose as we climbed into our beater. "Unwind the window," she said, "you don't smell so great."

When we got home, dad was sitting on the couch. Sara wasn't home.

"Kieran, I owe you an apology," he said.

"You owe *Sara* an apology."

He nodded. "I do. I already told her I was sorry. She's out shopping with my penance."

He was bribing her. Great.

"How's your dirt bike?"

"It's fine."

"Sounds like the carburetor was running rough."

"I'll fix it." I didn't need his help.

"Perhaps we should go look at the new models in the city. Make a day of it."

"What?"

He smiled. "Come on, Kieran. The dealership has a new Turbo Kawasaki. You should take it for a test drive."

"Seriously?"

He grinned. "I had a good month. You deserve a reward."

How many times had he lied to us? A hundred times? A

thousand?   But every time we think, 'Maybe this time he's changed. Maybe this time he'll come through.' Every time we're wrong.

Maybe this time, though?

~ 12 ~

I showered and changed, and we went. It was fun. We admired bikes. I even got to ride a couple. It was like flying. I wanted one like crazy, but I knew better than to ask. Seriously, I didn't need a new bike. I needed a new life. I needed money for college. I needed a sister who wasn't about to produce a mini-jock.

The air conditioning on Dad's truck wasn't working, and it was hot out. We were both sweltering on the drive home.

"Let's go in here," Dad said, pulling into the nearly empty parking lot of a sports bar.

"I can't go in there. I'm under age."

"Nah. It'll be fine. Jed runs this place."

Jed was one Dad's old friends. He was a one legged, ex-con with three ex-wives. Dad always seemed to know what bar he was tending. Twice when I was a kid Dad had left me out in the parking lot while he went inside to 'have a talk with Jed.' Once I'd waited two hours. Once it was four. That time, Sara was in her car seat. It had been cold, and I'd had to dig a filthy, tattered, stinking dog blanket out of the trunk to drape over us. We'd huddled together, watching the clouds our breath made until we fell asleep. A social worker had woken us up hammering on the window.

Dad moved out after that.

We sat in a corner booth in the nearly empty bar. Jed limped over and slapped Dad on the back in greeting. "About time you came to see me!"

"A pitcher of your best on tap," Dad announced, grinning, "for this fine young man and me."

Jed didn't even ask for my ID. He just headed back to the bar, grabbed a pitcher, and set it under the tap. "So how's life in Fort Mac?" he asked Dad.

"Profitable. You should head up there. You'd make a fortune."

Jed laughed. "I like my climate milder." He set the pitcher on the table, and put mats and mugs beside it.

"You're getting soft," said Dad, reaching for the pitcher and pouring us each a mug.

"I'm tired of rough life. I've got a comfortable girl, a comfortable job, and a comfortable house. You should try it."

Dad laughed. They started to reminisce about their youthful adventures which seemed mostly about drinking, driving too fast, and other times they should have died, but didn't.

I tuned them out. I inhaled the beer. It was sweet and pungent. I sipped cautiously. It was cold and golden. I tilted the mug and drained it.

Dad grinned as he talked to Jed, and re-filled it.

I stared at the mug, then turned my attention to the football game playing on the big screen. I drank and watched. I imagined riding a turbo dirt bike through the hills, far from my troubles. I watched the players running like ants across a striped green sock.

The mug never seemed to empty. Three more pitchers were delivered to the table.

Dad played pool with a couple of guys who challenged him.

There was laughter, groaning, and shouting.

I watched the football game as the players wove their way unsteadily across the field. When they were tackled, I closed my eyes. It hurt.

Eventually, as the quarterback fell to the ground, I groaned, and tipped onto over with him into blackness.

When I came to, it was to find Jed and Dad tugging me to stand. I staggered out to the truck.

A hammering woke me up. My eyes were glued together. I forced them apart, and squinted from the white hot glare they revealed. I shut them again. It was so hot, that it was like being in a beer steam bath.

"You're drunk," Sara announced.

"I never get drunk," I muttered. My voice echoed painfully in my head.

"Then why are you sleeping in Dad's truck, stinking like a brewery at seven in the morning?"

I swallowed. My tongue felt hairy.

She hit the button and unlocked my door. The click sounded like a grenade going off under my ear. I groaned.

"Come on, stinko. Let's get you into a shower."

"You can't lift me. You're pregnant."

"Yeah, well, then I guess you'd better walk yourself, hadn't you? Come on." She pulled my arm and I squinted through the narrowest slits I could make and still see something. I unfolded my legs and slid them onto the ground. I waved back and forth like a flag pole in a hurricane.

Sara giggled. "I've never seen you drunk."

"I'm not drunk. I don't drink. Remember?" I squinted down at her. "You'd better not drink, either. It's not good for babies." I stretched out to put a hand on her belly. It seemed like I reached for miles until I found it. "You'll turn its brain to lace if you drink. I've seen pictures. Don't drink!"

"I am not drinking, Kieran. You did. Get inside before you ruin your reputation as the sober, responsible kid." She smirked at me, and tugged harder.

I took one unsteady step and then another, guided by her firm arm on my elbow. "There you go. Good job!" she said. She pushed me into the bathroom, and shut the door. "I'll call the dairy and tell them you're too sick to come to work today," she said. She sounded just like Mom.

I stared at the water in the toilet, and suddenly I was desperate to pee. I reached down to undo my fly, but I couldn't make the zipper work. My fingers couldn't find the pull tab. I fumbled, cursing my fingers, the zipper, and my dad. Then I pissed myself.

I stared at the yellow puddle underneath me. I folded onto the floor, tears dripping off my chin, piss burning my leg. Disgust rose in my throat. My mouth not having a pull tab, I stuck my head in the toilet, and vomited my self-revulsion. I was my father all over again.

~ 13 ~

"Can I buy you an ice cream cone, handsome?"

Chancey was smiling from the door of the cafe looking like a goddess in cut offs and a halter top. I glanced around to see who she was talking to and she laughed, "I'm talking to you. You might as well come in; free ice cream isn't on offer every day."

I probably wasn't going to be good company today. I still had a headache, and my stomach was unsteady. Worse, my mind was unsteady. Was I doomed to become my father? He was gone when I'd gotten up. Mom had scowled at me and muttered, "Good riddance to him," so she wasn't feeling forgiving today either.

Chancey said, "Well? Are you coming in?"

It was a little weird having a girl offer to buy me something, but she was cute, and it was hot. I gave a little nod and went in after her.

A few minutes later we were walking down the road, licking our ice cream cones.

"So when is your sister due?"

"How'd you know...?"

She laughed. "We were on the beach, handsome. I'm guessing five or six months?"

I nodded, "Yeah, six."

"Is the guy around?"

"No."

She grimaced. "It's tough when they take off. You feel really alone. It's good she has her big brother to look after her. I wish I'd had one."

It took me a moment to realize what she was telling me. My tongue froze mid-lick and I studied her over the top of my rum raisin. I tried to make my voice neutral. "You have a baby?"

She nodded. "Yeah. His name is Rowan."

"How old is he?"

"Almost two."

She was so skinny it was hard to imagine that she had ever been big enough to have a baby.

"Does he live with you?"

"Yeah. There were no other options."

"Why not?"

"My mom divorced my dad when I was four. She re-married nine years ago, and has been trying desperately to have a baby ever since. She did the fertility treatments and the whole bit. No baby. Then I got pregnant. It was almost as if she wished that baby right into my uterus."

She glanced over at me and laughed. "You're blushing. Does talk of uteruses embarrass you?"

"No." I lied.

She took the last bite of her cone and dropped the napkin into a garbage can. "Do you want to meet him?"

"Who?"

"Rowan."

What was I supposed to say? Little kids kind of scare me, to be honest. Especially really little ones. They seem sort of fragile, they walk around in their poop, and they scream a lot. They're cuter when they're about kindergarten age, when they are a lot sturdier. I didn't want to seem like a jerk though, so I said, "Sure. That'd be cool."

She grinned and turned toward the channel. "We live down here."

"In those new condos?"

She nodded. "My parents just bought it to have as a summer place."

Summer place. Sheesh. Three story beautiful stone condos on the channel with double garages. They were bigger than my house and a whole lot nicer. She was way out of my league.

She turned into the complex and then paused, giving me a strange look. "Are you okay? You look sort of green."

"They're really nice."

"Yeah, so?" I saw the light bulb click on over her head. "Handsome, don't hate me because my parents have money."

I shrugged, feeling stupid.

"Look. My parents are home, so I need to call you something besides 'handsome' or they're going to wonder if your mom is some kind of tripped out hippy."

Now I felt *really* stupid.

I muttered it as she opened the door.

The condo was even fancier inside. My whole house would fit inside their open plan living room. The floor at the entrance was black rock, but the rest of them were dark glossy wood. There was a fireplace covered with river rock. The ceilings were really high and the place was flooded with light. I froze. Chancey gave me a little nudge and I sort of stumbled into the living room. On the right her kitchen was gleaming with stainless steel appliances. "Holy." I whistled under my breath. "What does your winter place look like?"

Suddenly there was a squeal and a knee high blur flew past and attached itself around Chancey's legs. "Hey, Sissy."

"Hey there, little man! I brought someone to meet you."

Rowan peeked out between his arms and then buried his head in her knees again. She laughed and peeled him off, lifting him into the air and blowing raspberries on his belly as she walked into the living room. His giggles filled the room. She tossed him onto the couch and he howled gleefully, "Again!"

A lady appeared in the entrance of the hallway. "Hi, Chance. Who's your friend?" She looked like one of the women on the rich housewife shows.

Chance was tickling Rowan. "He's Kieran. A genuine year-round local, believe it or not. This is my mom, Sybil."

Her mom nodded at me, and I reached out to shake her hand. "Hello, ma'am."

Sybil gave a twitch of a smile as Chancey continued, "We're going to take Rowan to the park, if you don't mind?"

Rowan squealed again and ran to the door.

Her mom laughed, "He'll enjoy getting out. Get your shoes on, honey."

It took a few minutes to get the shoes on the correct feet. Rowan's happiness made it way harder than it could have been.

Rowan took Chancey's hand and then reached up to offer me his other one. I took his little hand in mine, and we walked, arms swinging.

Rowan was chattering the whole time, but I couldn't really understand what he was saying. Chancey did though, because every once in a while she'd answer. We came to the highway across from the arena and Rowan shouted, "Sissy! Park!" He pulled his slippery hand out from mine.

A semi-truck came rumbling past and my heart stopped.

SHAWN L. BIRD

"Rowan. No!" said Chancey. She had a firm grip on his other hand, and his burst of speed just curled him into her. "Hold Kieran's hand. The road is dangerous."

Very solemnly, he reached his hand back to me and said, "Sorry, Sissy."

She gave his hand a squeeze. "It's okay. Let's cross now."

As we came to the edge of the park, we let him go and he ran to the equipment. Chancey sat on a bench.

I stood beside her and watched her watching him. "He calls you Sissy instead of Mom?"

She scowled. "My mother's idea. We just let people think he's my little brother. It saves a lot of trouble."

"Kind of ironic."

She nodded. "Yeah. She wanted a baby, but I wasn't allowed mine. I understand, but sometimes it ticks me off. I love him. He's my son. I would like to be allowed a little more say in his life, but I understand that they think it's for the best. I'm free to be a kid." She got up and picked up Rowan to help him grab the monkey bars, and supported his weight as he grabbed hand over hand concentrating hard.

"You're a good mom."

She smiled. "Thanks. What's your sister going to do?"

I shrugged. "She doesn't know."

"But you're there for her?"

I exhaled slowly, "Yeah." Whatever it cost my dreams, I would be there.

~ 14 ~

Sara was so huge by the end of the summer that it looked like she'd stuck a beach ball up her shirt. There were times when I still couldn't believe any of this was happening. Today I was taking her into the city for pre-natal class.

I grabbed the keys off their hook while Sara sat staring blankly at the kitchen table.

"Well? Are you coming or not?"

She didn't move for a moment, and then she said quietly, "It hurts."

"What hurts?"

She rolled her eyes at me. "I'm having contractions. They hurt."

My stomach dropped to my knees. I stared at her. "Contractions?" I whispered, panic rushing through me."

She looked over at me with a grin, "You've gone very pale all of a sudden."

"Yeah. No shit." I took a deep breath, my mind racing. The baby was coming. "Okay. Let's get you to the hospital."

She giggled. "No, they're not *those* contractions."

"What other kind are there?"

"These are called Braxton-Hicks contractions. They're practice contractions. The real ones are much stronger and will be way more painful, apparently. I still have another month before the baby is coming. Don't worry." She eased herself up belly first, and reached for her purse. "Let's go."

My heart was still pounding as we climbed into the car. The baby was coming. It was coming *soon*. In a month or so, I'd be an uncle. Me. Wow.

Sara was watching the lake below us. "I can't believe I'm having a baby," she said, absently rubbing her belly. Then she grinned and glanced over at me. "Can you take a hand off the steering wheel?"

"Why?"

"He's moving."

"He?"

"Well, maybe not 'he,' but I would rather say 'he' than say 'it.'"

Sara gently lifted my hand and set it high on her belly, on the shelf it made beneath her breasts. It was weird. She was my sister. I don't think I'd touched her belly since our last tickle fight when she was like ten or something.

"Just wait."

The highway was quiet, and we drove along on the vividly blue day, the lake sparkling below us, with my right hand resting nervously across her belly, and then *bump*, something rolled under it. I pulled my hand off as Sara laughed.

"Was that you?"

"No. That was him. He was telling you hello."

As if a magnet was drawing it, I set my hand back, and sure enough there was another rolling bump under my hand. This time I didn't take my hand off, and the rolling turned again. It was cool.

"Hi, baby," I whispered.

I put my hand back on the wheel. I could feel the silly grin on my face.

"Pretty cool, eh?"

I smirked, "Yeah, Sara. That is pretty cool." I felt like I'd been smeared with happiness. Sara having a baby was not a good thing. No kid her age should be having a baby. And yet, that baby couldn't help who his parents were. A baby deserves to be welcomed whatever the circumstances of its arrival. Suddenly all I hoped for was that it was healthy, that my sister had been eating well enough and kept off all the crap so she hadn't poisoned the little guy. I met her eyes and we smiled at each other.

The bellowing wail of a horn echoing around the bend was the first warning.

The second warning was the screeching of its air brakes.

There was no third warning; there was just a semi-truck sliding down the road, the cab in the north-bound lanes, the trailer in the south-bound lanes ready to sweep away everything in its path.

Everything happened in slow motion after that. I hit the brakes. Sara screamed. Our car and the semi-trailer were like toys being pulled together by giant children. I gripped the steering wheel and turned it. There was really nowhere to go except over the edge toward the lake. That wasn't much of an option.

The car spun around to the right heading toward the edge; the trailer was coming right for me, and then the world went black.

When I woke up everything was white.

There was humming and swirling movement everywhere. I tried to focus on something but I couldn't make images settle into anything solid. There was screaming somewhere. Sara's voice shouting something. Wailing.

Then darkness again.

~ 15 ~

I woke up once to whirling lights and a paramedics calm voice. I woke up again in emergency. The third time I woke up, I was in a hospital room with sun streaming through the window. Mom was reading a book in the chair beside me.

"Hi," I said.

She jerked, and then smiled down at me. "Welcome back."

"What happened to Sara?" I was taking inventory of all my body parts. I seemed to have everything, even if every inch hurt.

"She's fine."

"The baby?"

"He's fine, too."

"He's here?"

Mom nodded, "The accident started labour early, but everything went well. Thank heavens for air bags. It could have been horrible." She glanced at her watch. "I have to get to work. I'm glad you woke up before I had to go." She bent over and kissed me. Her eyes glistened with tears.

"Can I see them?"

She nodded. "They're on the other side of the nurses' station. A nurse will wheel you over there. I'll ask one to come in. I'm so glad you're awake." She kissed me again, sniffing back tears as she waved good-bye. When you're poor like us, you don't miss

work even if your kid is at death's door. I understood why she
had to go.

A nurse came. She helped me, and the assorted plastic tubes
and bags attached to me, into a wheel chair. I was able to wheel
myself, slowly, down the hall.

A middle-aged couple was standing outside the window to
the nursery, looking in nervously. They met my eyes, as the
woman went inside to talk to the nurse.

"Are you a new father?" asked the man.

I shook my head. "I'm a new uncle."

"Ah." He looked relieved.

"You?"

He nodded, "Yeah. Hopefully."

That was a weird thing to say. Either you are a father or you
aren't, right?

His wife appeared at his side, glowing. "The nurse says the
mom hasn't signed the papers yet, but she's pretty sure it will
happen. I saw the baby. He's gorgeous, Jason!"

Jason put his had on her shoulder solemnly, "Don't get too
excited Meredith. You know that nothing is sure until forty-eight
hours after she's signed."

She nodded, "I feel good, Jason. I think this time we will
have our baby." She wrapped her arms around him, and I met
Jason's eyes for a moment and saw the fearful hope there.

I wheeled into Sara's room, but she wasn't alone in her little
curtained corner.

"What are you doing here?" I said, brows lowered.

Ryan shuffled his feet and glanced anxiously at Sara's
sleeping form. "I have a right to see my baby."

"Do you?" I glared at him, then glanced covertly over to Sara. Her face was a little bruised, but it wasn't too bad, all things considered. "Where were you for the last eight months?

He grunted noncommittally and looked at Sara. "Why is she so fat? I thought she had the baby."

"You are an ass." I said.

"Hey, now. That's not nice."

"You thought she was going to walk out of here in her skinny jeans, did you?"

Ryan's eyes shifted between me and Sara. "Well, yeah. She had the baby, right? Or is there another one in there?"

"Why are you here, Ryan?"

"It's my baby."

I cocked an eyebrow at him.

He sighed. "Legally, I mean. I have to sign the papers, if she's giving him up."

"Ah. Did you?"

"Yeah. I thought I'd tell her I'm sorry, but she's ignoring me."

"She's sleeping, dude."

"You think so? Since when does Sara sleep in the middle of the day? She's a party animal!"

"She just shoved a baby the size of a watermelon out of her body. We were just in a car accident. She's entitled to a little sleep."

"Oh." He looked at her, eyes fluttering in a dream, or perhaps in an effort to keep them closed. "Well. Tell her I stopped by, okay? And that I'm sorry. The baby's cute."

Tears were beginning to pool in the corners of Sara's eyes, but she kept them tightly closed.

"Okay. She'll be glad you signed the papers."

He grunted.

"And Number Eight?"

He glanced back over his shoulder at the doorway. "What?"

"Next time, wear a condom, eh?"

He grinned. "Right."

The tear began a voyage down the side of Sara's cheek as Number Eight sauntered out of the room.

I wrapped my hand around hers, careful not to disturb the IV in her wrist, and gave it a gentle squeeze. "He's gone."

She squeezed back, but she didn't open her eyes.

With my other hand, I picked up a magazine and flipped through it absently, glancing up at her now and then. Her breath evened out and I think she really did fall asleep eventually, but it wasn't long before the door opened and a nurse came in pulling a wheeled bassinet. A squirming bundle was making funny noises.

"Is he hungry?" I whispered.

The nurse smiled, "Yes, but he might be satisfied with a little snuggling first if you want to let her sleep a little longer. Do you want to pick him up?"

She must have seen the panic in my eyes because she grinned, "Here, it's easy. Hold under his bum and here under his neck. Don't let his head slip back; he's too little to hold it up himself yet."

Little mud coloured eyes looked at me. I couldn't look away. He was hypnotizing me or something. He studied me, and I studied him. I realized I was jiggling him gently. I didn't know when I'd started that.

"He's cute, eh?"

I looked over to see Sara watching us from the bed, her head still on the pillow.

"Yeah. Are you going to feed him?"

She tightened her lips and shook her head as she closed her eyes again.

"You're going to let him starve?"

She shook her head again. "Take him back to the nursery. I have to let my milk dry up. I'm not keeping him. They gave me something to stop the milk, but I can't feed him."

I looked at her huge breasts. My little sister could produce milk. Gross. I shook my head to clear the image and considered her words. "When did you decide that?"

"I've thought about every scenario I can come up with, and this seems like the only option that makes sense for the baby." She sniffled. "I have to go to school. I want him to have a good life. We barely scrape through every month. It's better that I let someone who already has an education and a good job look after him."

I looked at his sweet, peaceful face as he looked back at me. "But how can you stand not knowing where he is for eighteen years until he's old enough to look for you?"

"No, it doesn't have to be like that. I'm going to have something called an open adoption."

"Huh?"

"I got to choose the parents. When he goes to live with them, they'll send photos and news about him every few months. It might work out that I can go to his birthday parties and graduation and all that stuff. He'll just have two families."

I stared at her.

"What?"

I shook my head in awe. "You're the bravest person I've ever met, Sara."

"I'm not brave. Brave would be risking everything and trying to raise him myself. I'm not brave enough for that. Just thinking about it terrified me."

"It's brave Sara, because you have to have a lot of trust to give away your baby. It's an amazing gift you're giving that couple."

"I'm counting on that," she nodded. "It always feels good to give someone a gift they really want, right? It feels better to give the gift than it does to receive it." She sniffed very quietly, and then whispered again, "I'm counting on it."

~ 16 ~

And so here we are a year later. I'm celebrating on the mountain. It's quiet up here, and it's quiet inside my head. I haven't wanted to punch anyone since I hit Dad on the beach. His bad choices don't have to influence my life any more.

A doe steps out of the forest, and then a speckled fawn follows her.

"Hello, beautiful." I whisper. They watch me, but then they begin to nibble on the clover. Motherhood has made the doe brave, and her baby feels secure.

Chancey was back again this summer. We lay on our backs and watched the falling stars here in this clearing on top of the mountain. I send her a text to tell her I'm thinking about her, and she texts back, "XOXOX."

She makes me smile.

Sara is dating Davie. He promises she won't be getting pregnant.

There was a settlement from the accident. It is a huge relief. There's food on the table, and the rent is paid. Mom still works two jobs, but she is saving the money to go to college.

I am going to college, too. I can't believe it. Mrs. Sykes got me into an apprenticeship program. I'm learning how to be an electrician. I can't believe how well it pays. I'm getting credit for both high school and college, and it's free for the first year. How crazy is that?

We see Dillon every month. He's starting to crawl. Whenever we come, his eyes sparkle and he stretches his arms towards us. It makes my heart warm. Jason and Meredith are great parents. He has a big back yard and Jason is building a huge play structure. Sara and I laughed so hard at that. I mean, Dillon can't even walk yet, but they have big dreams for him. We have big dreams for him, too. Sara was courageous enough to put him on the path. I was lucky enough to be his uncle. It is a big responsibility. I want him to be proud of me.

Number Eight has vanished into the mists. I heard that he received a high check that has put him on the injured roster this year. He isn't coming to play here, at least. If there is any justice in the world, I hope karma ensures he's out for good, but he's talented, and he probably will end up in the NHL someday. Sara says she watches the girls giggling in the halls and ogling this season's hockey players. They look at her and can't imagine they'd ever be stupid enough to end up pregnant. Sara says she looks at them and wonders which one will get caught this year. There's always one. She figures some girl will come up to her quietly on the way home from school one day, and she'll listen to a tale of woe with no surprise at all.

Life in Laketon 3

CHANCEY

~ 1 ~

"Do we have to leave?" I groaned, staring around my room at the huge stack of stuff I had to somehow get into my suitcase.

My mom came in and dumped the contents of a laundry basket onto the bed. "All vacations end," she said with a sympathetic grin.

I waved my hand at the now immense pile on the bed. "How could all this possibly fit into this little case? It defies the laws of physics."

"If you didn't shop while we're here, it would be less of a problem." Mom sank onto the head of the bed, where the stack was low, and exhaled a deep sigh. "I hate packing, too."

"Can't I just leave these clothes here? I'm not going to wear summer stuff in Calgary. It'll be winter the week after school starts."

Mom laughed. "You'll have outgrown it all by next year. This way you can pass it along to Dana."

Dana was my best friend. She is two sizes smaller than I am. Way to rub it in, Mom. "I could go to school here. You know there's a high school. All those kids working in the stores go there. Why can't I?" Our summer condo would be perfectly fine to live in all year. Several of the other residents did. There was no reason we couldn't, too.

"Our jobs are in Calgary." Mom laughed. "Sorry, Chancey. Summer ends for all of us. However…" She rummaged in her pocket and handed her a flyer. "I saw this at the grocery store this afternoon. You want to go? It can be your seasonal farewell to Laketon."

I studied the mini-flyer. It was a photo-copied quarter page with a silhouette of dancers and music notes that announced an all-ages dance at the renovated purple barn that served as community centre for the summer village of Laketon.

"I can go to this? Alone?"

"I don't see why not. You're old enough to stay out of trouble, right? Brian needs to get the boat in, but it'll only take the two of us."

"You're sure?"

"The cashier told me most of the town goes to these dances. Kids to grandparents. Seems safe enough, don't you think?"

"You just want some private time with Brian while I'm kept busy." I raised an eyebrow and tried to wiggle it.

Mom laughed, "Well, there is that. How else are you going to get a little brother or sister?"

"Ew, Mom. Gross." Mom and Brian had been married for five years and had spent the last year in a determined baby-making campaign.

My phone beeped and I glanced down at the text.

"Dana?" her mom guessed.

"Yup."

"Get this stuff put away." She dropped the laundry basket at the door. "Anything you don't want, put in the basket and I'll drop it off at the thrift store on our way out of town."

I read Dana's message and sighed.

Went out with Rick last night. I am in love!

Rick was a grade above us. He had dreamy dark curls and worked out. In the last year, he'd gotten seriously hot.

Mom stood up, "What's the news?"

"Dana is going out with Rick."

"Do I know him?"

I shrugged. "I don't think so."

"Is he nice?"

"I guess. He's really cute."

"Cute is okay, but nice is better. I'm happy for Dana, if she's happy, but remember honey, you don't need a boy in your life to be complete. You are a capable, beautiful, intelligent person. You don't need anyone else to be happy."

"Says the woman who gushes and giggles worse than a kid whenever Brian walks in the room." I tried to keep the tinge of mocking out of my voice.

Mom's eyes twinkled. "All right. That's fair, but it took a horrible first marriage to learn I was strong and able. Those qualities were what attracted Brian. A man who respected my strengths was attractive to me." She smirked and added, "and those biceps were attractive to me."

I snorted.

Mom chuckled, "I know you don't believe me, but you'll see. A partner who kindles your fire rather than smothering it makes all the difference."

Another text notification binged.

"You'd better talk to Dana before she freaks out." She left, calling back, "Don't be long. Dinner will be ready in a bit."

We have so much in common! Dana had written. **We went to The Beasleys concert and talked for three hours afterwards at Pizza Pizzazz.**

I fought down a stab of jealousy. The Beasleys were just a

local band, but they were cool.

Jealous. I typed back. **Going to a dance tonight,** I added, so I didn't sound completely pathetic.

When do you come home? Can't wait to see you and tell you everything!

We leave tomorrow. Sucks to go back to real life. But it'll be good to see you.

School Monday. Summer went so fast!

Right?

Did you get your summer romance?

Way to dig it in, Dana, I thought. **Tell you when I see you!** I added a raised eyebrow emoticon.

Oooh! Way to torture me!

I laughed and hoped that by the time I saw Dana I'd actually have a romance to report. **Dinner now. C U soon!**

I stared at the screen at a duck-face selfie of Dana in her work uniform. Rick was behind her, making rabbit ears above her head. They were a cute couple.

When we'd left for Laketon in June, Dana had challenged me to find a summer romance, but the hot days had lulled me into believing I had time. I had spent the entire summer in Brian's boat. Mom called it 'idyllic existence' and 'adventure everyday.' I called it tedious, but I didn't have the energy to go off by myself. It wasn't fun without Dana.

Most summers Dana came to Laketon with us, but this year she'd gotten a summer job.

Mom and Brian still gushed and mooned over each other like newlyweds, so I felt like an extra in my own house. Where was my romance? I was nearly fifteen!

Meanwhile, there was Dana, working in Calgary, and now she and Rick were going out. Dana was getting a romance, and it could keep going through the school year since Rick went to their school.

I read through their conversation again. I was the loser who was last to find someone who liked her. Even Mom had beaten me to new romance. But I had one last chance.

Tonight at the dance, I'd see if I could find adventure, if not a romance.

~ 2 ~

I didn't usually dress up in the hot Laketon summers. No one did. Baggy t-shirts and shorts were the uniform of the entire town. But tonight I was determined to stand out. I needed an outfit that announced that I was up for an adventure.

I dug out a tight black t-shirt dress that barely covered my bum, and after some consideration, slipped into bootie shorts for the sake of modesty.

"We're off to pull up the boat!" Mom called up the stairs.

"Okay!" I called back, thankful I didn't have to hear Mom's opinion on my outfit. She probably wouldn't care, because she was cool that way, but she'd be bound to say something embarrassing.

"Be back by ten!" Mom added.

"Okay!" The dance started at six. I'd have four hours. That was plenty of time for an adventure wasn't it?

I went into Brian and Mom's en suite bathroom to hunt for her make-up bag. I normally just wore lip gloss, but some dramatic eyes could maybe make me look older, more interesting. I pulled up a 'smoky eye' tutorial on my phone and followed the instructions. After a couple of abortive attempts, I got the hang of layering up the colours with the brush. I lined my eyes in black and added three coats of mascara. I added some blush and a shimmery pink lip gloss.

I rummaged in Mom's closet for a cute pair of low strappy sandals that would work with the dress and ensure that I would be able to dance. Heels might have been nice, but I had to be realistic. I had to walk to and from the dance, after all.

I slipped on the sandals and stepped back to study myself in the full-length mirror.

The effect was definitely dramatic, even if the eyes weren't quite symmetrical. I didn't look like myself at all.

That was a good thing.

I wondered if the kids I'd seen on the beach would think I was new. With these dramatic eyes, I looked like a mysterious cross between Goth and actress.

Add in the tight dress and there was no disguising that I was a girl, that was for sure.

Perhaps it was all a bit much for Laketon? I twisted in the mirror, studying all angles.

No, I decided. Tonight, drama was perfect.

This was my last chance for adventure.

I slipped some money in the pouch on the back of my phone and tucked the phone into the strap of my bra.

Ready.

My heart pounded just walking down the condo stairs. It felt like the world was tipping off its axis. Why did it feel like everything was about to change?

I practised walking. I tried shoulders back, but that felt like I was presenting my boobs for inspection, and that was just weird.

I tried a rocking motion in her hips that made my butt swing side to side. That was quite fun. A car-full of teens drove by and someone wolf-whistled loudly, cutting the air. I jumped and followed their laughter down the street. They were going to The Purple Barn, too.

Finally, I imagined a string tied on the very top of my head, tugging my back upwards, the movement elongated my spine, tucked in my pelvis, and lightened my step. Ballet dancer walk. Yes. Very confident.

This was the walk of a girl ready for adventure and romance.

This was the walk of someone who was worth knowing.

I arrived at The Purple Barn certain that I couldn't look any better.

"Hey!" someone called from the steps of The Purple Barn. A tall boy with sandy brown hair, about my age waved.

I looked around, but he seemed to be talking to me.

"You coming in here?"

I inclined my head. *Play it cool*, I thought. Then I added to myself, *but not too cool. Don't be a snob*, so I smiled at the boy and said, "Yes. I am. How much is it?" I already knew it was five dollars for singles and twenty dollars for a family because it said so on the flyer, but I had to say something. I was beside him on the step now.

"Ten bucks," he said, sticking out his hand. "You can pay me."

I raised an eyebrow and glanced over his head at the sign. "It says five."

He glanced over his shoulder. "Damn. Caught." He grinned. "Pay Judy over there at the table. Save a dance for me?"

He blinked innocently at me and I laughed. "We'll see." Always better to keep them guessing a bit, isn't that what they always say?

I paid my five dollars, got my hand stamped, and went into the barn. On the stage, a band was settling into place, but they hadn't started playing yet. It felt weird to be at a dance without Dana. At home we did everything together.

She'd challenged me to find fun and adventure this summer, and what a woeful job I'd done of it. *Last chance, Chancey*, I thought to myself. *Make this dance count!*

Around the room people were gathered in groups or pairs, chatting. I helped myself to the glass of punch that my admission included and wondered how long it'd be before someone spiked it.

"Hi," purred a deep voice behind me. "Haven't seen you around here before."

I turned and blinked at the stunning guy standing there. Tall. Dark wavy hair. I swallowed her punch and gave him a smile I hoped didn't look as wobbly as it felt. "I've been around," I shrugged. "You weren't paying attention."

A slow smile broke across my face and his eyes shimmered. "Got a name?"

"Yes," I said, and turned away from him. I took two steps, glanced over my shoulder and said, "Later." I walked—*think like a ballerina*—to the doors and stepped out onto the cool step. The band had started playing and the music masked her quivering breaths. *Be cool. Be cool.*

"Hey," said the boy with the sandy brown hair. "Ready for our dance?" he put out a hand.

"Why not?" I said, grabbing his hand and laughing as we joined the crowd on the dance floor.

"I'm Danny!" he shouted into my ear over the thudding bass. "Nice to meet you!"

"I'm Chancey! Do you live here in Laketon?"

"Yup. All my life." The dance stopped and we panted a bit as we walked over to get a glass of water. "Where are you from?"

"How do you know I'm not from here?"

"You're kidding, right? We all start in kindergarten together in Laketon. There are only a hundred and fifty kids in the elementary school and fewer in the high school. We know everyone. Are you a mystery?"

"Guess so."

The tall dark guy slid between them, "Danny, introduce me to this lady of mystery."

Danny's eyes narrowed, as if he was considering his options.

"You don't need to know my name," I said, freeing Danny from the responsibility.

"Sure, I do," the dark guy purred, doing something with his eyes that made them smolder dangerously.

"No," I said, lowering the register of my voice. "You don't." Playing hard to get was more difficult that I'd imagined.

Beside me, Danny coughed.

One side of the dark boy's mouth quirked up. "Well then. I guess you don't need to know my name either, right?"

I rolled her eyes and glanced to Danny. "Do I?"

Danny smirked. "Definitely not." He stuck out his hand, "Another dance?"

But before I could reply, the other boy pushed Danny's hand away. "You had your chance. This dance is mine. Come on, mystery girl." And he pulled me out onto the floor.

He could dance. Like, really dance. I had never met a boy who could dance so well. It was swing tune, and he spun me, flipped me, and I whirled from arm to arm as if I were some kind of top. I didn't know the steps, but I didn't need to. I felt like I was on one of those reality shows. As the song ended, he dropped me into a dip and I blinked up at him, dazed and amazed.

People around us were grinning. An old couple applauded.

"Still want to go back to dance with Danny?" he said casually.

"Um." I had no voice. "Water?" I croaked.

He grinned.

He set his hand at my back and steered me past the refreshment table, and out the door, grabbing a couple of water bottles on the way out.

"You should use the cups," I murmured. "Bottles are bad."

"Honey, bottles are neutral. I'm bad."

I laughed, still breathless from the dancing, and maybe from the heat of his hand, and maybe from the promise in his voice that he was offering an adventure, if not a romance.

"Come to me, mystery girl," he said, pulling me off the deck where other couples were standing, fanning themselves and talking.

We burst through the doors. I pulled back a little as he tugged me off the deck. "Where are we going?"

He laughed. "I know some comfortable seating, come on." He stopped at a pick-up, tossed the water bottles in, and crawled over the back. He reached out his hand, "Up."

I set my foot on the bumper and he pulled me into the box, where we collapsed in a heap on an old couch that precisely fit the width under the cab window. "Why do you have a couch in your truck?"

"Usually for the drive-in. It's actually a hide-a-bed," he smirked. "Wanna hide?" He reached his arm around me and pulled me tight against him.

"I don't…" I squirmed a bit, but he pulled me closer. "Come on, baby. You know you want to."

I reared back and stared at him. "Did you just use the most exhausted cliché in the English language to try to persuade me to make out with you?" I threw my head back and laughed, moving away from him while he was surprised. I wanted an adventure, but this was a little much.

I glared at him. "I don't even know your name. You don't even know mine."

"Ah, but I know you are poetry in my arms," he purred.

"Oh, please." I rolled my eyes, but he wasn't looking at me any more.

There was thump on the side of the pick-up behind me. "Problem here?" asked Danny casually. He glanced over his shoulder at a couple of his friends who were standing behind him a little way off. "I think it's time she danced with someone else." He looked at me, "Want to come meet my friends?"

I looked between dancer boy and the other three. They were just regular looking young guys in t-shirts and cut-offs. They didn't seem as dangerous as dancer dude, so I reached for the ledge. "Yeah, I think I do." I scrambled over the back of the truck and jumped down next to Danny.

"Thanks," I murmured to him, as we headed back into the barn.

"No problem. I might not be a fantastic dancer, but I'm not an ass-hole like him." He glared behind him and yelled, "And get out of that truck!"

"Do you know him? I don't think I've seen him before." I glanced over my shoulder, to where dancer guy was watching me. I was sure he would have burned himself in my memory if I'd seen him on the beach.

From the truck box, he lifted a water bottle in an ironic toast to me.

"No, he's not from Laketon, but he comes to the dances now and then." Danny looked at "What do you girls see in him?"

I shrugged and without thinking said, "Sex appeal?"

Danny snorted. "You know, that isn't even his truck. It belongs to my brother."

"Is it really for the drive-in?"

"Yeah."

"Is it a hide-a-bed?"

"No. Just a regular couch. Look, let me introduce you to some of my friends. There are other people to hang out with here. Safer people. Some of us can even dance a bit."

We showed our stamps as we went back into the barn. A girl with a riot of blonde curls came up to them. "Who's this, Dan?"

"Cherie, meet Chancey from Calgary. Cherie, introduce her to the gang, eh? Keep her out of trouble."

I watched him go. "He's a real knight in shining armour, isn't he?"

Cherie laughed, as she handed me a cup of punch. "He must like you. Or he's growing up."

"What?"

She watched him weave through the crowd. "He's my little brother."

I sipped my punch. Still not spiked.

Cherie took me to a gathering of girls and I spent the next couple of hours dancing and laughing with them. I kept expecting to see the dancing guy, but he didn't show up.

At ten minutes to ten o'clock by the clock above the refreshment table, I smiled at everyone and said, "I've got to get home. I promised my mom I'd be back by ten."

"Are you walking?" Cherie asked.

I nodded. "Yeah. It's just a few blocks. I'll be fine."

The girls exchanged glances. "You know what?" said Cherie. "I feel like a walk. Shall we join her, girls?"

Just like that, I had my own squad.

"You don't need to do this, you know."

"Don't be silly. We haven't seen your dancing admirer for a while, but that doesn't mean he isn't around, looking for opportunities. Danny thinks he's trouble, and while my brother isn't the smartest cookie in the box, he has a pretty good sense for trouble, he's been in enough of it. Girls should never leave other girls to become a statistic, my mom says. We have to look out for one another. Too many bad things happen to us."

"But it's Laketon!"

She snorted, "Small towns aren't as safe as you might think. Trust me, we need to look after one another."

We were already half-way to the condo. "That's nice of you," I said. "I appreciate it."

Not a minute later, we heard the crunch of tires following behind us. "Hey, beautiful!" called the dancing guy from an old sedan. "Ditch the crew! I'd be happy to take you home!"

"I'm good, thanks," I called over my shoulder. My heart was pounding again.

"Look, I'm sorry I scared you. I'm not actually a bad guy."

"Take off, creep," snarled Cherie. "She's not interested!"

"But she *is* interested," he said, softly. "Isn't that right? She's just a little nervous, but I can take care of that. I'll be gentle."

Cherie whipped out her phone and snapped a picture of him. "Marie, get his licence plate." Another girl went behind the car. In BC, licence plates were on both ends of the car. He was from Alberta, then. Or perhaps just his car was.

"I'll get out and pose, if you prefer?" He leaned his shoulders out the window and turned his head, still driving the car forward ominously close to them, "This is my better profile."

"What are you on?" Cherie shouted, reaching her arm out to pull me protectively against her. "Didn't you hear us? Get lost!"

He laughed, "Fine, fine!" pulled his shoulders back through the window, revved the car, and drove off, spitting gravel back at us.

We had reached the condo development.

"This is me," I said, waving an arm at the complex. "Thanks for the escort. I guess I did need it after all."

Cherie nodded, "He's cute, but he is *definitely* trouble. Will we see you around?"

"Next summer. I leave tomorrow."

"All right then, see you then. Stay away from creeps!" she said as they waved and headed back to the barn.

I glanced over my shoulder and hustled up the steps of the townhouse. "I'm home!" I called as the door shut behind me.

A muffled noise that I hoped was a greeting came from upstairs.

The lights were out in the living room, but a strip shone out from under the door of Brian and Mom's room.

"Did you have fun?" Mom called.

"Yeah, some local girls walked me home."

"I'm glad you made some friends."

"Yeah, me too." I wasn't going to tell her why. "I'm going to have a bath. See you in the morning."

Her reply was muffled and choked off with giggles. I didn't want to think what that was about.

I ran a bath and crawled into steaming bubbles. The washcloth was soon black from mascara and eye shadow. I leaned back in the hot suds and thought about the night.

It had been an adventure, and while parts of it had been scary, had I actually been in any danger? Surely, not? What would have happened if I'd kept kissing dancing dude? Was he as good a kisser as he was a dancer? My body tingled as I thought about it.

Next time, I'd kiss first and worry later. Next time, I was going to make a romance as well as an adventure. Next time, I wasn't going to pull back.

Dana might have a boyfriend, but she wasn't going to have all the fun this school year.

Mom was doing the dishes when I came home from school three weeks later. I tossed my backpack onto the floor and opened the fridge, waiting for her to shout at me for not taking off my shoes. She didn't.

I poured my milk and went into the pantry for chocolate syrup. I reached past her for the spoon, waiting for her to look at me, and tell me chocolate milk was too much sugar, and that I was going to spoil my supper. She didn't.

I sat at the table in Brian's spot and studied her as I stirred the syrup into my milk and took the first sip.

Her elbows were sunken in the wash water, but she was just staring out the kitchen window. I enjoyed a few more sips, but the pleasure of breaking a house rule was lost when no one noticed it.

"Mom?" I said, finally. "Are you okay?"

She inhaled with a quivering sort of gasp and cleared her throat. "Oh, yes. I'm fine, Chance. How was school?"

"Fine."

"Did you have your audition? How did it go?"

"The audition was last week. I told you, remember?"

"Oh." Her voice was very small. "Right."

"What happened, Mom?"

Her shoulders were heaving.

I finished my milk. "Mom?"

She sniffled and whispered. "There's no baby this month."

"Bummer." I tried to sound deeply saddened. I kind of was.
She and Brian had been talking about in vitro fertilization if
Mom didn't get pregnant soon. The $10,000 procedure would
pay for a really nice car for my sixteenth birthday. I wasn't as
keen on a baby in the house as they were. "Did you tell Brian?"

She nodded.

This meant Brian would be late coming home. Brian knew
that being at home today was going to mean being drenched by
my mother's silent tears. It was just as stressful for him as it was
for me to cope with Mom's agony. She would weep, and weep,
and weep. After a week or so of weeping, she would get
extremely cheerful. I would have to wear ear plugs to bed to
avoid the embarrassing thumpings coming from their bedroom,
and we would all pretend everything was fine for three weeks
until she got her period again.

"Will Brian be working late tonight?" I asked, even though
I already suspected the answer.

She tightened her lips and nodded.

"Right. So, I...um...promised Dana that I'd come to her
house tonight to work on our lines for the play." I glanced over
to the stove, in the unlikely event that there was dinner lurking
somewhere in or on it. I did not see anything promising. "Should
I pick my own dinner up on the way?"

Mom sniffed. "I'm sorry, honey. I'd planned to make a
lasagna tonight, but the time got away from me."

Of course, it did.

"That's okay." I rummaged in my bag for my script and
pulled my coat back on. "I'll be home around eight, okay?"

She cleared her throat and set a plate into the drying rack, "Yeah. Sure."

I shut the door behind me and breathed with relief at my escape.

My mother was inconsistent in her grief. Sometimes she needed me at her side and made me look at my baby pictures while she wept beside me. Sometimes she wanted to watch horror movies and shouted curses at everyone on the screen. It was not pleasant however she chose to deal with it.

Washing dishes in super slow motion was new, and maybe the creepiest thing yet. I didn't want to watch her self-destruct. Mom's are supposed to be stronger than that.

I walked over to Dana's house. Dana had been my best friend since grade three. It was easy being with her. Dana was also, unfortunately, very attuned to my mother's menstrual cycle. When I got to her house though, there was a strange car in the driveway. I hesitated a moment, but then I tapped lightly on the back door and let myself in.

Dana was being engulfed by a pair of broad shoulders and a shock of black hair. I coughed as the door shut behind me, and Dana squeaked, pulling away.

I smirked at her, as a blush rose on her face. "Hi, Rick." I said, as I grabbed an apple out of the fruit bowl.

Rick blushed, too. "Um. Yeah. Hi Chance."

"Since when have you two been making out in kitchens?"

"Shh!" Dana hissed, glancing furtively behind her. "My dad will hear you!"

"If your dad doesn't think you're alone with a boy and you're not making out, he deserves to live in his ignorance"

"Huh?" Rick grunted and wrinkled his brows. "What does that mean?"

I laughed. Rick was stunning to look at with his model good-looks and black curls, but he was never going to be on the honour roll.

Dana rolled her eyes.

"What's going on?"

"Another month. Another crushing blow for my mom."

She grimaced. "You should come out with us. We're going to see that new alien movie that everyone is so excited about. You know, the one with Damien Dillon."

Damien Dillon was delish. I looked at Rick. "Don't get any ideas about making out with both of us in the dark theatre."

He immediately blushed scarlet and looked frantically over to Dana. "I wouldn't!" he gasped.

Dana smacked me in the arm with a laugh. "Don't torture the poor boy. She looked thoughtfully at Rick. "Do you know someone who'd like to join us? You know, to keep Chancey company?"

"I don't need a pity date, Dana," I growled.

Rick pulled out his phone. "This is perfect! I'll call Simon."

I was immediately intrigued. "Who's Simon?"

Our school was big, but if any available guy was called Simon, I'd have known. I loved the name Simon. I had a major crush on a character called Simon Templar from an old black and white British series called *The Saint* that Brian and I watched when Mom was out for an evening. Simon was suave. Handsome. Intelligent. There was definitely no Simon at Morgan Heights.

Rick shrugged. "He's my cousin. He just moved in with us for a while. He's not in school."

This was getting better and better. I looked at Dana, and asked with my eyes, *Had she met him?*

She shrugged. That meant no.

Rick hung up his phone. "He was free. He'll meet us there."

I wasn't so sure about the concept of a blind date, but there was no way I was going home, so I texted mom, "Going to movies with Dana. Back 10:00." She'd check her phone when I didn't get back at 8:00, and then she'd cry some more. In the meantime, I'd be snuggled up to Rick's gorgeous cousin. With luck, he'd have a British accent.

~ 5 ~

There was a line at the theatre, and the three of us stood shivering in the cool autumn air, waiting to get inside. I kept looking around. "What does your cousin look like?"

"Like me, sort of" grunted Rick with a shrug.

"What does that mean? Does he have dark hair? A cleft in his chin? Dimples?"

Rick shrugged again. "He's taller than me." The line moved forward. I looked around, but there was no sign of anyone arriving who looked like Rick.

"He won't stand you up," Dana said. "I hear he's desperate to get out of the house."

"Why? Has he been on house arrest?" Dana and I giggled, but Rick tightened his lips and looked up at the posters as the line finally made it through the doors into the lobby.

"What? *Has* he been on house arrest?" I asked.

"No." Rick muttered, "of course not." He didn't meet my eyes, though.

"Hey!" snarled a voice from the other side of the room, and a huge kid elbowed his way toward us. He must have weighed close to three hundred pounds, his face was covered with acne, his hair glistened with oil in the fluorescent lights, and he looked seriously mean.

I gave a panicked look over to Dana, whose eyes were also wide.

"Excuse me," the big guy said as he pushed past us and butted into line with his friends, a few people ahead of us.

I closed my eyes and inhaled with deep relief. When I opened them, I looked at a broad chest. I tilted my head up, way up, and met laughing eyes. They were the most incredible shade of green, like a spring tree in bud. It was the dancing dude from Laketon.

"Hello there," he said. "You must be Chancey." His voice was low and sultry. It made all the hair on my body stand up. He was better than I remembered. He was the most gorgeous thing I had ever seen. He looked like Clark Kent, all tall and brawny. His dark, wavy hair even had the curl in the middle of his forehead tonight.

I opened my mouth to answer him, but I had no words. I closed it again. Then I opened it, again, and made an incoherent little squeak.

He glanced over at Rick. "Doesn't she talk?"

Rick rolled his eyes.

I tried again, "Yes," I squawked. Now I sounded a bit like a chicken, "Hi Simon." I swallowed and cleared my throat. "I'm Chancey." I tried to smile in a sexy sort of way.

He grinned and wrapped an arm around my shoulder. "Oh, I *sincerely* hope so." He showed not the slightest glimmer of recognition.

In my jeans and jacket, with nothing more than lip gloss, far from Laketon's Purple Barn, he didn't know we'd met before.

I glanced over at Dana and she winked at me, standing behind Rick as he ordered popcorn and drinks.

Simon didn't buy anything. I'd have liked popcorn and a

pop, but I didn't want to shake his arm off to stop at the counter. We just followed behind Rick and Dana as they went to find their seats in the theatre. We picked out a spot against the wall in the back row.

The lights went out, and Simon's hand moved from my shoulder to hover above my breast. I stiffened. I wanted to say *Whoa, Dude!* but I stopped myself.

I had decided the next time I had a chance with a cute guy, I was going to be braver. This was even better. I was getting a second chance with dancing dude himself. Simon. I savoured the name.

Tonight was the night to stop being the safe, predictable Chancey.

I inhaled and pushed my chest upward toward his hand.

My body was alert, every hair tingling upright as he stretched his fingers to brush across my nipple. It puckered to attention as I held my breath.

What was I doing?

I exhaled as the screen filled with the previews.

Simon leaned over nuzzled his nose into my hair, breathing into my ear.

I squirmed away, giggling as the air tickled.

In front of us, someone hissed, "Shhh!" My nose was full of popcorn. Someone nearby had nachos.

As the movie started, Simon pulled me closer.

I wasn't going to let him take the lead. I was an adventurer tonight!

I turned to him and in the flickering light from the screen, I saw his eyes gleaming. He was interested in me. Even without the skin-tight dress and dramatic make-up, he wanted to get to know me.

Screw it. I stretched up and kissed his lips.

He made a guttural groan or surprise and kissed me back, wrapping his arms around me.

‑ Wow. Could he kiss!

I had been kissed before, but I'd never experienced anything like this. When he pushed my lips apart with an insistent tongue, my heart was pounding as I kissed him back breathlessly. I did not see a single scene of the movie.

As the credits rolled, he pulled me to my feet. "Come on!" he said, and I followed him out of the theatre feeling like I was in a dream. In the lights in the lobby, he looked even more like actor Damien Dillon. He was my own leading man. He was so gorgeous! I felt impossibly lucky, like I'd won some sort of lottery.

He pulled me close to him and we kissed again.

My lips were sore and tender from two hours of this, but I wanted more.

Simon broke away and laughed into my eyes. "You are too awesome, Last Chance!"

"Whose Last Chance? I'm an opportunity!"

He stretched his arm over and squeezed my breast, right in front of the line up for the late show. "Oh, yes you are!" he purred into my ear.

My cheeks flamed, but I elbowed him in the ribs playfully.

He laughed again as he manoeuvred us through the doors.

Dana and Rick followed us, holding hands.

Outside, Simon kissed me again, then unwrapped himself from me, and nodded at Rick. "Thanks for the invite. See ya around, Last Chance."

Just like that he was gone. I blinked. It felt like the sun had just gone out. The crowd around us thinned, and Simon was on the other side, heading down the street.

Dana said, "Does he always come and go so dramatically?"

Rick shrugged. "He has his own way of doing things. Are you all right, Chancey?"

"Huh?"

He laughed and nudged Dana. "We'd better get her home. She looks like she might fall into a coma or something."

"Har har," I said, trying to drip some sarcasm off my swollen tongue. "I can't help it if Simon likes me."

Rick grunted, "Right."

Dana elbowed him hard in the ribs. "Just take us home."

He drove us back to Dana's house. The street lights were a kaleidoscope of colours. I couldn't focus on anything.

My head was swirling. I had a boyfriend! A boyfriend who was the sexiest thing I'd ever seen, and he couldn't keep his hands off me. I felt a surge of warmth rush up my spine, like I was super-charged.

"Come on, Chancey. We're here." Dana poked my arm. "I'll walk you home." She gave Rick a quick kiss through the driver's side window and tugged at my elbow. "Let's go."

I was floating down the road. I couldn't stop smiling through my swollen lips. They were going to be so chapped tomorrow. I didn't care.

"Chancey..." she began.

"Isn't he *gorgeous*?" I said, beaming at her. "I can't believe I'm going out with someone like that! I wonder what kind of car he drives?" I imagined the sporty little Volvo from the old TV show and sighed.

"Chancey, maybe Simon isn't quite who you think he is..."

"Right. Maybe I'm the Queen of England. Did you *see* him?"

Dana sighed. "Would you like to review the plot of the movie, in case your mom asks?"

I giggled at her practicality. "Yeah. You'd better tell me."

She gave me a quick synopsis. She finished just as we got to my house. The lights were still on.

"Good luck with your mom."

I gave her a quick hug and ran to the front door. I'd never been so happy in my life, and on the other side of the door was my mother, who was probably still crying. I tried to clear my face and opened the door.

~ 6 ~

Mom and Brian were snuggled together on the couch. Brian was watching TV looking over her head resting on his chest. Her eyes were closed. I wondered if she was asleep.

"Hi, Chancey," he said quietly. "Did you have a nice time?"

I tried to make my face as neutral as possible, "Yes."

Mom opened her eyes. "Ooh, baby. You look flushed. Are you sure you're not coming down with something?"

"No. I just walked home with Dana. It's cold outside."

"Ah." She closed her eyes again and pushed her head into Brian's chest. He patted her shoulder absently, as he watched me.

"What movie did you see?"

"*Dark Side of the Mist*. It wasn't very good, but that Damien Dillon is a great actor." I let my eyes go dreamy. I was thinking about Simon rather than Damien, but they didn't need to know that.

Brian snorted. "If you like that creepy, fake-plastic look."

I scowled at him and he laughed. "Oh, I see. You like dolls?"

"I like him," I said firmly. "I'm going to bed."

Mom opened her eyes again. "Are you sure you're okay?" She struggled to sit up. "Let me feel your forehead."

"I'm fine, Mom," I groaned, but I went to her, and let her put the back of her hand on my forehead. She would keep nagging if I didn't.

She furrowed her brow thoughtfully. "I don't know. Something isn't quite right." She gazed into my eyes, then glanced over to Brian. "Look at her eyes."

"What?" I said.

"Show Brian your eyes."

I turned to him and widened my lids. "What's wrong with my eyes, Mother?"

"Do they look bright to you?" she said to Brian.

"Hmm." Brian said, in a completely non-committal way.

"Do you think she's on some kind of drug?"

"Mom!" I shrieked. "I am NOT on any drugs! Good grief!"

"Fine, fine." She looked at Brian again, then back to me. "I'm sorry. Something's strange, though. You must be coming down with something. You'd better get into a hot bath and get to bed early."

"That was the plan." I muttered, heading upstairs to my bathroom. I ran the water and imagined Simon here. My nipples rose in memory of his hands, and I stared at them in the mirror. My face was pink, and my eyes were sparkling. Simon brought out the best in me, and why not? He was the perfect guy! I added some bubble bath to the water.

I pulled out my phone and texted to Dana, **Thanks for inviting me tonight. It was amazing!**

She replied, **Talk tomorrow.**

I plunged into the hot bath, bubbles puffing around my chin. I closed my eyes and saw Simon's eyes laughing into mine. I could almost feel his tongue moving through my mouth.

There was a knock at the door, "Chancey? We're off to bed.

Good night!"

It was barely ten o'clock. I was going to need my ear plugs tonight. Mom wasn't wasting any time moving onto the next month's project, apparently.

I lowered my head into the water, tuning out the world. When I lifted my head out, I could hear murmuring from Mom and Brian's bedroom.

"Maybe we should consider adoption," Brian was suggesting.

That was brave of him.

I couldn't quite make out Mom's strangled reply, but I could imagine her face.

"No, no, honey!" Brian continued, "Don't cry! Of course, I'm not giving up yet, but you need to start considering other options. This hasn't been going well. Perhaps it's time to look at..." His voice trailed off.

Mom was crying loudly now. Her choking sobs were coming through the wall. I dropped my head back under the water to drown them out.

My phone buzzed on the floor by the tub, and I surfaced to read, **Simon wants your phone number. Should I give it to him?**

I gave a little hoot and sloshed the water as I lunged to grab the phone. I typed, **YES!!!!!!!** then I leaned back and felt myself glowing. Who said love at first sight didn't exist?

I stepped out of the tub and toweled myself off. I massaged body cream in, imagining Simon's hands. My nipples rose again, along with goose bumps all over my body.

My phone buzzed again, and my heart started to pound. I picked it up and stared at the screen. **Hey Last Chance. Add me**

My hands were shaking so hard that I had trouble putting

his name into my contacts. I should answer him. What should I say? My heart pounded even harder. I was finding it difficult to breathe.

Through the walls I could hear the springs of Mom and Brian's beds bouncing slowly up and down.

I typed, **Done.** I wanted to type, "I love you!" but thought that might seem a bit pushy. Obviously, he liked me, but there was no point being completely crazy.

The phone buzzed again as I was brushing my teeth. My body tingled all over as I read **Ur hawt. C U around**

He thought I was hot! He couldn't spell, but I could live with that.

I slipped into my pyjamas and started shaking as I climbed into my bed.

How should I reply? "Thanks" seemed silly. Finally, I typed, **C U** and put my phone under my pillow, damn the fire risk. It kept a little bit of Simon beside me. I closed my eyes, put earplugs in to block the sounds coming from Mom and Brian's bedroom, and imagined his tongue in my mouth, his hand cupping my breast. My whole body quivered with happiness as I drifted into dreams.

~ 7 ~

I waited for Simon to call or text me again, but whenever my cell rang or buzzed over the next few days, I grabbed it, and sagged when it wasn't him.

Finally, I gave up, and I texted him. **Hey you! Hope you're having an awesome day!** Then I waited, heart pounding, for little tone that meant a text had arrived.

Nothing.

Dana saw me staring at my phone. "Don't call him."

"Who?" I said, feigning innocence.

She rolled her eyes. "Don't call him. Don't text him. If he's interested in you, he'll call."

"What if he doesn't know I like him? What if he's shy?"

"How could he possibly not know that you like him? He spent two hours with his tongue down your throat. If you weren't interested in him, you're a slut."

"Hey!"

"But you DO like him, right? So, you're not."

"Right," I glared at her. "I'm not."

"So, wait patiently. You don't want to be pushy."

I pouted. "I don't want to wait."

"That's obvious."

I sat down in a huff. I acted as if I were joking, but I was sort of serious, too. I thought about Simon all the time, imagined his kisses, wondered if he liked me as much as I liked him, dreamed of being wrapped in his body. I sighed.

My phone rang, and after a glance at the screen I grinned up at Dana. "Ha! It's him!"

His text said, **How can my day be awesome without you in it? Wanna go out tonight?**

I grinned over to Dana. "He wants to take me out."

"You're sure that's what he wants?"

"What else would he want?"

"Sex?" she said bluntly.

"Simon is not after some random hook up. He's not like that!"

"How would you know? Have you had a conversation of more than four sentences yet?"

"You're just jealous."

"I have Rick. Remember?"

"Simon is better than Rick."

Dana laughed. "You don't know enough about Simon to know whether he is or not. But that doesn't matter. When is this date?"

"Tonight."

"That's not a date. That's a booty call." Dana shook her head. "Have some self-respect. Don't go."

"If I don't go, he might not call me again."

"Then he isn't worth going out with today. Don't do it, Chancey."

I scowled at her, and texted back. **What time will you pick me up?**

Dana looked over my shoulder as I hit send. She sighed. "Oh, Chance. I hope he's not just using you."

"You need to stop dissing him. You just don't know him the way I do. He's amazing. Trust me. This is going to be the start of something great."

"I sure hope so." She leaned in and gave me a hug. You deserve good things, Chance. Don't under-estimate yourself."

"What are you talking about?" I said, as my phone buzzed again. I turned away from Dana to read it privately.

Meet you at the C-train station at 11.

I scowled for a moment.

"What did he say?" Dana asked.

I shrugged. "I'm going to go home so I can get ready. See you tomorrow."

At the door, she said, "Don't do anything I wouldn't do." She tried to say it jokingly, but her eyes were wary.

"I'll be fine, Dana. Don't worry."

She waved as I left, but the worried expression in her eyes didn't change.

It was just eight o'clock when I got home.

Mom looked up from a magazine she was reading on the couch. "Hey, honey. Did you have a good day?"

"Yeah."

"Do you have any homework?"

"Yes. I'm going to have a bath and get started on it. I'm really tired tonight." I made my way to my bathroom, smirking to myself. I was finally going to see Simon again! As I ran the bath water, I imagined his arms wrapped around me, I could feel his lips. The thought of him made me happy all over. It would have been better if he had come to pick me up, maybe at a time when I could introduce him to my mom and Brian, but this was okay. I was glad to be able to spend time with him, whatever we were doing.

I stepped into the bath and imagined the kids at school seeing me with Simon. They would be so amazed! There was no one nearly as gorgeous as he was at our school. Well. Maybe Rick was close, but Simon was taller and more muscled. And he could dance. I wondered how often he worked out. I wondered when our next school dance was. How fun it'd be to be to see everyone's shocked expressions as we danced!

I scrubbed and soaked for half an hour, but I actually did have some homework I needed to get done, so I drained the tub and got to it.

At nine o'clock I heard Mom coming up the stairs. She knocked on my door, and stuck her head in. "Almost done?"

"Yup," I said, shutting my math book. "Just finished. How are you doing?"

She shrugged. "I'm fine. Thanks for asking." She glanced over her shoulder and smiled at Brian.

Uh oh. I was going to need ear plugs again tonight.

"Good night, Hon.."

"Night Mom. Night Brian."

They headed off to their bedroom and I turned the radio on my old alarm clock.

Through the wall I could hear Mom giggle, so I put in my earbuds. I grabbed the novel I was reading and tried to ignore the noises coming from down the hall and working past the music coming through my earbuds and the night talk show on the radio.

Finally, things got quiet.

I looked at my phone. It wasn't quite ten o'clock yet. I scrolled through Simon's messages. There were only three of them, but they made me sigh happily. Nobody I knew had a boyfriend as interesting as he was.

He was mysterious and cool, just like a handsome spy in a novel. He had so much sex appeal it made me drool just thinking about him.

And Simon liked *me*.

I checked my phone again. Ten thirty. I turned my doorknob slowly and stepped into the hall. The radio still throbbed behind me, now it was a Top Ten countdown show. It masked my steps. I snuck up to Mom and Brian's bedroom door and listened. No sound.

I went back for my wallet and jacket, turned down the music enough that if they woke up, they'd think I'd fallen asleep while masking their sounds of romance. They were used to me doing that sort of thing, and they wouldn't bother to come in to turn it off if they got up in the middle of the night.

I slipped on my shoes, eased open the back door, and set off to the C-train station.

~ 8 ~

It was cool outside, and I pulled up the hood and burrowed my hands into the pockets of my jacket. I walked quickly to try to generate some heat. It was peaceful out. The windows were all black on my street, except the Davidson's on the corner. They had a new baby and the nursery lamp glowed faintly through the pink curtains. I wondered if someday Simon and I would be up late cuddling a baby in our own nursery. The thought made me smile as I rounded the corner and moved into a jog.

There was a group of guys outside the pub. One called out, "Hiya, babe! Wanna party?"

Another laughed and shouted, "You're not man enough for a pretty lady like that. Come on, sweetie pie. You shouldn't be out here all by yourself. I'll take care of you!"

My heart pounded. I kept looking forward and moved a little faster.

The C-train station was lit up, and there were cameras there, so it was unlikely that there'd be any trouble, but I did wait in front of a camera, just in case. The encounter outside the pub was unsettling, because while the guy was undoubtedly drunk, he was right. I *shouldn't* be out here by myself.

"Boo!"

I squealed and my heart exploded out of my chest and into

my throat.

Simon laughed, and wrapped his arm around me, squeezing me, as he leaned down to kiss me. "Hey, Last Chance. Ready for an adventure?"

"Sure," I said, when I got my breath back. "What are we doing?"

He grinned. "Train coming!" He hadn't stopped to buy a ticket, which was weird, but maybe he had a pass like I did. He led me onto the platform as the train pulled in. "We're going downtown, where the action is."

There was no one on the train when it pulled in.

The protective drunk from outside the pub sauntered up the platform with determined casualness, as if he was trying hard not to show that he was having trouble walking in a straight line. "Is this guy bothering you, sweetie pie?"

"No." I said, looking away from him.

Simon kissed me again, thoroughly.

The drunk coughed. "That's very rude behaviour," he said. "A gentleman should be more respectful of his girl."

Simon's smile spread slowly, and he kissed me again, forcing his tongue deep into my throat. I tried not to gag. It wasn't very romantic making out in a train in front of a drunk. He lifted his head and levelled his gaze at the drunk, daring him to say anything again, but the drunk just shrugged.

"You're sure you're okay with this guy, sweetie pie? He seems a trifle lecherous."

He seemed genuinely concerned, so I smiled at him. "It's okay. Thank you for your concern."

"All right then," he said, moving to the door so he was ready for the next stop. "You have a good night, ya hear?"

"Good night," I replied as he left the train.

"What a loser," Simon said, setting his hand on my breast and kissing me again.

I wiggled my head out from under his. "Is it much farther?"

He buried his head again and bit at my nipple. It hurt.

"Hey!" I flicked at his hand and he came up laughing. It didn't make his eyes twinkle in merriment, though. He looked... Sort of purposeful. Determined. It made a tingle run up my spine.

"Here," he said, standing, as he grabbed my hand and pulled me after him. We're getting off here."

There were actually people on the platform here, but most of them looked inebriated. I wondered if sober people ever came out at this hour. Simon pulled my hand and dragged me down an alley. It smelled of piss and vomit. I pulled back.

"What?" Simon's brows were down.

"It stinks down here! I don't want to go there."

"It's fine. It doesn't stink inside."

"Promise?"

He grinned, and this time his smile did light his eyes. "You're going to love this. It's right here. Come on, Last Chance."

He was indicating a shiny red door. He jiggled the door handle, but it was locked.

My heart dropped a little, but he knocked, and it opened a crack. Soulful music came out the crack, too.

"Hey Robin! It's me, Simon. Can my friend and I come in?"

A hairy head poked out of the crack. Little black beetle eyes peered out between long dark wavy hair and a bushy beard that looked like it was heading to his waist. He looked me up and down and grunted. The door opened, and Simon and I ducked under Robin's arm and into what turned out to be a club.

They didn't seem to believe in the non-smoking ordinances, because people were smoking all over the room in deep leather-vinyl booths. Girls carrying small drink trays were wearing tiny skirts and tinier shirts. They didn't worry about ages of the clientele either, since no one seemed at all concerned with us. I don't know, maybe Simon was actually old enough to be here, but I sure wasn't, and it was weird that no one seemed to care.

"A gin and tonic for me," Simon said to a cute little blonde in a pink micro-uniform, "and a Singapore Sling for the lady."

"What's that?" I asked, as the waitress left.

"Girly drink. You'll approve."

"Gin and tonic?"

"Manly drink. I approve." He grinned.

A band made its way onto the stage and settled in. The soulful canned music stopped, a big guy started beating out a rhythm on the drums, and suddenly the club was full of music. Brilliant music. Astonishing music. Music that reached into my brain, dived into my belly, and wallowed around. It made me want to move, it made me want to sing, to dance, to cry, and to sleep all at once. "Oh!" I gasped.

Simon smiled. "Incredible, eh? I thought you'd love them." He wrapped his arm around me, and I nestled under his shoulder, endeavouring to sip my pink drink without stabbing myself with the little umbrella.

There were just five instruments: a baritone saxophone, a soprano saxophone, the drums, a clarinet, and a trumpet. They were winding tunes around themselves and spinning them into the air. This was a mix of jazz, blues, heavy metal, and rock. It was familiar and new. It was simple and complex.

The drink made me feel pleasantly warm and lazy. The music made me feel alive. Simon made me feel electric.

Between the three of them, I was enclosed in a bliss that I could
never have imagined. I was with a man I loved, having an
adventure so wonderful it was almost a dream. Simon met my
eyes and kissed me again. My body throbbed in response.

It was nearly three o'clock when Simon pulled me to my
feet. "Come on, Last Chance. Time for us to get on the
homeward journey. He waved to Robin the doorman, and we
walked, swinging our hands in a blissful revelry.

"Have fun?" he said, grinning at me.

"Oh, yes. That was fantastic. How did you know about this
place?"

He shrugged, "Connections." We walked up to the C-train
platform. There were a few drunks around. I didn't see anyone
who was sober, except the security guard who stood by the
elevator. His eyes were suspiciously blood shot, though.

The screen announced the next train and Simon let go of my
hand. "Thanks for coming out tonight. I'll text you later."

"You're not riding home?"

"No, I've got somewhere else to go. Here's your train. Bye!"
He gave me a little shove as the doors opened, and I
automatically stepped through them.

"Simon..." I began, but he grinned and spun on his heels,
heading for the stairs before I could finish.

A very smelly man sat at the seat behind me and leaned
forward as if he wanted to talk. I opened my phone and opened a
book app. While I pretended to read, my attention was
constantly scanning the creepy passengers.

How would Simon feel if I was murdered on the ride home?
Would he regret just pushing me onto the train and abandoning
me?

He had somewhere else to be, though. Maybe he was

volunteering at an old folks' home or something,

I didn't meet anyone's eyes as I got off the train, and headed home. There wasn't anyone hanging around the pub now.

On my street, even Davidson's nursery light was off. I slipped quietly in the back door and slid the lock bolts home. I took off my shoes and crept quietly into my bedroom. The house was silent.

I set my stinking clothes in the hamper and crawled between my sheets. I was asleep before I could even set the alarm.

~ 9 ~

When Brian woke me up at seven o'clock, I felt like my eyes were glued closed.

"Whoa, he said. "You don't look so good. Are you sick?"

I struggled out of bed, "I have a math test this morning. I'll be fine."

I got to school more or less on time. I wrote my math test, and probably passed. I kept sneaking worried glances at my phone all morning, wondering if Simon had texted and I'd missed it.

At lunch Dana came and sat with me. "We should probably talk about Simon," she said.

"Isn't he great?" I sighed. "I can't believe we're going out."

"Yeah. About that..."

Rick muscled in between us at that moment, grinning at Dana. "Are you going to help me with that math like you said?" Apparently, he hadn't passed the math test.

She glanced over at me, and then shrugged, "Sure. Of course. You don't mean now?"

Rick was pulling a folded piece of paper out of his pocket. "Yeah. I couldn't figure out the answers to these three questions.

My phone, tucked under my bra strap, started to vibrate. "I'll talk to you guys later, okay?" I sped out of the room, looking for a private place to answer.

I ended up in the handicapped washroom. No one was likely to be hammering on the door. "Hi!" I said, as I turned the lock on the doorknob.

"Were you avoiding me?" laughed Simon.

"I had to get somewhere private. I didn't want anyone listening." I sat down on the toilet, fully clothed.

"Wise of you." He chuckled in rumbling bass that had my belly flopping like a fish was trapped inside it. "Where did you end up? I hope you're not stuck in a reeking janitor's closet or something?"

I laughed. "No. A nice little room with a lock, that's all." I double checked the lock was engaged.

"Look, I've heard word of a little event tonight. Would you be interested in joining me?"

"I..." I had a community theatre class tonight, but I would skip it to be with Simon. "I'd love to come. What time?"

"I don't know yet. I'll call when I know, okay?"

"Yeah. Sure. I'll be waiting for you."

"I'm looking forward to seeing you again, Last Chance."

"Me, too. I mean, seeing you." My heart was pounding so hard, it was hard to hear him. "See you tonight." I put the phone in my pocket. I was having difficulty breathing again. I looked into the weirdly slanting mirror, set for viewing from a wheelchair. If my mom could see my eyes right now, she'd be sure I was high. I *was* high! I was high on Simon! I couldn't believe he wanted me.

Dana was in the hall when I came out of the bathroom. "Why were you using that one?" she asked, brows down.

I shrugged, "I was in a hurry."

She shook her head, "We need to discuss that guy, you

know."

"Who?" I didn't know what she was so intent on saying, but I didn't need anyone bad mouthing Simon. He was perfect.

She rolled her eyes. "Fine. Be that way." The bell rang at that moment and cut her off. "I'll meet you at your place to go to rehearsal tonight, okay?"

"Oh. No. Not this week. I have a meeting to go to."

"Meeting?" she said, suspiciously, "Who are you meeting? You know that we're supposed to be working on that really tricky combination leading up to your solo part, right?"

"Yeah, but I really have to go to this meeting."

The vice-principal cleared her throat behind us. "Ladies? Don't you have some place to be?"

"Yes, ma'am!" We said in unison and headed to our classes in opposite directions.

I snuck out a back entry after school so that I wouldn't run into Dana. I raced home and changed, waiting for Simon's call. Then I changed again, and a third time. I wanted the perfect mix of sexy and...well...sexier.

Mom's car pulled into the driveway just as I had settled on my skinny jeans, a black bra and a sheer white boyfriend shirt. I took off the shirt and put on one of Brian's hoodies. It was excellent camouflage.

My phone buzzed and I leapt across the bed to check the text, but it was from Dana, **You sure you're not coming?**

I scowled at the phone.

Another text buzzed in, **Patty is going 2 B furious if you miss practicing your solo.**

Sorry. Meeting. C U tomorrow. I hit send with a purposeful whack of the key. So there.

Her reply popped back almost instantly. **If you're meeting**

Simon, don't. It's not worth it.

I stared at the phone with my mouth agape. Simon not worth it? It wasn't worth missing a rehearsal to be with him? Was she crazy? Simon was everything I'd ever dreamed of in a boyfriend. Of course, there would be sacrifices to be with him, but I would pay them. He was absolutely perfect. I wouldn't never have thought Dana would be jealous.

"Chancey! Dinner!" Mom shouted.

I adjusted the hoodie over my hips and headed into the dining room. It smelled really good. Brian came in from the family room and did a double take. "You're wearing my hoodie?"

"Yeah. It was in my clean clothes basket. Sarah must have put it there." Sarah was the housekeeper. "Did she make dinner?"

Mom nodded, "Sarah is a gem. What would we do without her to keep the house in order?" She set a steaming lasagna on the table and went back for the Caesar salad.

As she set it down, Brian raised an eyebrow and the salad tongs, "Other people manage to look after their own house full of kids, Meg. It's not like you're working all day." He chuckled as he put the salad on his plate and passed the bowl to me. Garlic wafted up from the Romaine lettuce.

Mom pouted in a cutesy sort of way, like she was just pretending, but then she started blinking back tears. She sniffed and looked away.

"I'm sorry, hon." Brian said, as he pushed his chair away from the table and wrapped his arms around her, rocking her gently back and forth. "I'm sorry. That was inconsiderate of me."

She shook her head and cried. I cut a square of lasagna and started to eat, ignoring them as they stood beside the table, arms around each other, rocking. Tears dripped off Mom's chin.

I chewed.

Mom sniffed, "Don't you have rehearsal tonight, Chance?"

The phone buzzed in my bra. I jolted. "Oh! No! No rehearsal! I'm feeling sick! I bulged my cheeks and pushed back my chair. I raced into the bathroom and leaned against the door while I dug under the hoodie for the phone.

I pulled it out to read, **Last chance...** my heart did a flip, until I noticed the rest of the message, **...for a ride to rehearsal.** It was from Dana. Damn her!

Where was Simon's message? Maybe he was dialing the wrong number.

I could hear someone in the hall, so I made gagging sounds, then flushed the toilet with a melodramatic groan.

"Are you okay, Chance?" Brian asked.

"No," I said weakly. "I'm going to bed." I kept my eyes down and shut my bedroom door firmly behind me.

~ 10 ~

I lay on top of the bed in my clothes. I looked at the clock beside my bed. Seven o'clock.

Why hadn't Simon called yet?

Was he hurt?

Had he been in a car accident this afternoon?

I stared at the ceiling, worrying.

An hour later, my phone buzzed, I grabbed at it, but it was just Dana. **Patty is pissed.**

Who cared? Simon was lying in a ditch somewhere.

I crawled under the covers aching. What had happened?

My phone woke me up. I grabbed it and read, **Ready?**

I blinked, what was I supposed to be ready for? Dana was being a bitch. Then I blinked and read the message again. It wasn't from Dana. It was from Simon.

Was I ready?

I typed, **Yes** and flipped the covers back as I checked the time. Eleven o'clock.

The house was dark and silent. I had to pee, but didn't want to wake them with the flush. The phone buzzed again. **Meet you at Crossroads Cafe in 15 mins.**

I gulped. How would I get there? It was only five minutes to drive there, but unless I jogged, there was no way I'd get there in fifteen minutes. I didn't want to risk having him change his mind.

Sure, I wrote.

I grabbed my coat and crept down the hall. The back door had two dead bolts. I tied my boots, and then slipped the bolts back as quietly as I could. I held my breath, straining to hear if there was any stirring in the house. I eased the door open and slipped outside.

It was cold. I started jogging down the road. I checked my phone. I was making quite good time, but I didn't want to arrive looking sweaty and ugly. I didn't want to be late, though.

I slowed and looked around. The streets were completely empty. I started jogging again.

When I got to the café, the lights were on, but no one was inside. I pushed in the door and headed right to the bathroom.

When I came out, a waitress was behind the counter. "Hi," she said, "can I get you something?"

I sat down at the counter in front of her, "Yeah, sure. Can I have a coffee? Double double."

She nodded and grabbed the coffee pot and a mug. "We have good muffins. Only a dollar."

"No, thanks. This is fine."

She shrugged and went back into the kitchen. I sipped the coffee and wondered what had happened to Simon. Had he been hit by a car? Had he been mugged?

I was just about finished when the bell on the door tinkled. "Hey, Last Chance."

My face split into a grin. "Hi!"

"Ready to go?"

I swallowed the last of my coffee. "Where are we going?"

He wrapped his arm around my shoulders. "Party. You'll

have fun. Come on."

I tossed a twonie onto the counter, and called out, "Thanks!"

The waitress said something that I didn't catch, and Simon and I headed into the night.

I looked around for Simon's car, but the lot was empty. "Where is it?"

"Not far, come on." He slid his hand down my arm and grabbed my hand. "Let's go!" He started running, dragging me along behind him.

I laughed, stumbling to keep up in my boots. "Slow down! What's the rush?"

He stopped suddenly. "You're right. What am I thinking?" He curled me into his chest and kissed me.

He smelled so good. His skin was spicy and smoky. My head swam, as he pulled his lips off my mouth. "Mmm. Chance, you are a lucky charm. Come on." He tugged me along, and I kept step. His legs were so long that to match his pace, I had to take two steps for every one of his. He squeezed my shoulders. "You are so adorable. Here it is, come in."

The house was kind of creepy. The siding was dark. There was a front porch, but it was missing pieces. The door was scratched up. The streetlight above us wasn't lit, so we were standing in a black hole of darkness. I could feel the throb of music coming from inside, but I couldn't determine a melody. No light leaked through any of the windows.

"There's a party here?"

"It's a private party. There aren't many people here, but don't worry. You'll be fine." He smiled down at me. In the light from the streetlight further down the street, his eyes were glowing, and when he kissed me again any doubts I had melted right away. When we came up for air I blinked.

He grinned, "You are damn sexy, kid."

I stuck out my bottom lip and blinked up at him in what I hoped was a sexy way. "I'm not a kid."

He raised an eyebrow.

"How old are you, Simon?"

He laughed and gave my shoulders a squeeze. "Old enough to know better, and young enough to do it again. Let's go." He opened the battered door, and we went inside.

It was dim. Simon guided me down the hall and then opening an interior door. "Watch your step on the stairs."

I stepped into darkness. There was a strange smell, kind of like incense. I stumbled a bit when I got to the bottom, reaching for a stair and being met by the floor instead. Simon grabbed my elbow. "Are you okay?"

"Yeah," I whispered. My heart was thundering. This was so weird, but in a cool way, of course.

Simon whispered in my ear, "Prepare for your doooooom! Mwa ha ha!"

There was an eerie glow beneath a door, and Simon pushed it open to reveal six guys, sprawled on chairs, couches and the floors, game controllers in their hands, all staring at a huge big screen TV. Other people were in corners around the room.

"Hey," said Simon.

"Shut the door."

He shut the door, "I brought a friend. Ethan, give her your chair."

A lump curled in a recliner grunted. "I was here first. Besides, I'm about to kill the dragon. I can't...arg!" On the screen, a tiny knight was devoured by a glittering scarlet dragon. "Women are bad luck in the gaming room!" He glared at me.

Simon laughed. "She's here to be my good luck charm. Shove over.' He squeezed onto a couch, reaching for a game controller with one hand, and pulled me down onto his lap with the other.

A haze of dry ice was drifting up from one corner and the blinking of a strobe light cast a surreal spell, like a haunted house. There were several couples in various corners of the room standing at a bar, curled on couches, and draped over each other on oversized floor pillows. A hypnotic rhythm was echoing around the space, pounding into my brain.

Simon squeezed my hand and pulled me up against him. He moved to the throbbing rhythm, and I moved with him.

Someone else came up beside us in the flashing darkness and whispered to Simon. He laughed and pushed me into other arms. I couldn't really see his face. He rubbed up and down on me as we danced. It was gross. I twisted my head to look for Simon. Between the flashes, I finally spotted him over at the bar.

In choppy movements like a silent movie, he approached and shouldered between me and my partner. He handed me a bottle, "Have a drink." I read his lips since I couldn't hear anything but the throbbing music. Perhaps he said, "This is pink."

"What is it?" I shouted over the music.

"What?" he yelled back.

"WHAT IS IT?"

He shrugged and pointed to his ear. He smiled and took a sip.

I shrugged back and tried it. It was sweet and fruity. I smiled and took a bigger swallow.

He dragged me over to an empty couch and pulled me down. He tilted his glass and chugged the whole thing down. I followed his lead. When my glass was empty, he took it from my hand, and leaned over and started kissing me. He started at my hand, and kissed all the way up the arm, all around the neck, and then down my chest and over onto my belly button. I pushed him off, giggling. Grinning, he came down to my mouth and we began kissing in earnest.

His mouth tasted of fruit: strawberry, grapes, peach, and pear.

His hands were everywhere, cupping under my butt, rubbing up and down my thighs, curling around my breasts. My body was on fire.

Then there was a vibration in my bra that jolted me.

My phone.

It was probably Dana.

I ignored it.

Simon's body was up against mine, and we were both panting slightly.

My phone buzzed again. "Damn it!"

I pulled slightly away from Simon and checked the screen. Text from Brian: **Your mother doesn't know you've snuck out, but she will if you're not back here in 15 mins.**

"Shit." I struggled to stand.

"What?" I read on Simon's lips.

I passed him the phone to read the text.

He gave me a twisted smile, shrugged, and led me across the floor.

Someone grabbed his arm and shouted at him, but I couldn't make out what he said.

Somehow, he found the door, and we made our way up the stairs and out the door. The irregular streetlights seemed dazzling after the surreal effect of the strobe.

"I'm sorry. I have to go or I'm going to be in serious trouble."

He didn't say anything, but we set off, jogging down the road. I felt dizzy, and I wondered again what the drink had been. We got to the café and he stopped. "Right. I'll let you go from here."

"You're not taking me all the way home? What if there are rapists and muggers out? It's two in the morning!"

He laughed and kissed me quickly. "Talk to you tomorrow, okay?" he said in a low, sultry voice that made my spine melt.

"Yeah," I drawled, my brain processing in slow motion. "Okay."

He spun in the opposite direction, and I tried to keep my pace to jog home.

The light was on in the kitchen.

I opened the back door quietly and stepped inside.

Brian was sitting at the kitchen table with a mug in his hand. He met my eyes and studied me. "Hot chocolate?" He pushed a mug toward my spot.

I sat down.

"Why don't I think you were out with Dana?"

I shrugged and sipped the hot chocolate. It was good, better than when Mom made it. Brian was very good at comfort foods.

"Oh. I know," he answered himself. "Because Dana is sensible and respects the basic rules of safety and security."

I shrugged again. Dana was not as perfect as he thought, but I wasn't going to disabuse him, in case he told her parents.

"So, where were you?"

"At a house," I said, keeping my eyes on my mug.

"With?"

I sighed. "My boyfriend."

"Oh? Does this boyfriend have a name?"

"Simon."

"Like The Saint?" he said, and he laughed.

I couldn't help grinning. "Yeah."

"Is he as handsome as The Saint?"

"Yeah," I said dreamily. "Even better. But he doesn't have the cool car."

I set down my empty mug and stood up. "Thanks for the hot chocolate."

"Chancey. It's not safe for you to go out like that. If something happened, we'd have no idea where to find you. Don't do it again, okay?"

I shrugged.

"I'm serious. If you don't want your mom to know, text me. But I'd rather you didn't sneak out at all. Any guy who wants you to sneak out to see him isn't showing you the kind of respect you deserve. I don't know your Simon, but so far I'm not impressed."

"Brian..."

He held up a hand. "I'm not arguing with you. I'm entitled to my opinion, and you're entitled to a boyfriend who respects you." He stepped forward and gave me a hug. "Go to bed. You're getting up in five hours. Sleep well."

"Good night, Brian."

"Good night, Chance."

I turned around at my bedroom door, and he was still in the kitchen, holding his mug, staring at the table.

~ 11 ~

"Come on, Chancey." Dane wheedled. "Your mom will let you sleep over at my place, won't she? It's my birthday!"

"I don't know. I think she's suspicious that something is going on. Brian knows about Simon, but I don't think he trusts me yet."

Dana pinched her mouth thoughtfully. "Please?"

"I'll ask. It'd be fun to sleep over. It's been a while"

To my surprise, Mom didn't mind. I think she was planning a romantic evening with Brian, and she was happy to have me out of the house so they could run around naked and have sex on the kitchen table, or whatever it was they did on their romantic weekends. I didn't ask them for particulars.

Brian studied my overnight bag. "Stay out of trouble, eh?"

"Of course."

Mom laughed, "Chancey always stays out of trouble, don't you?"

Brian raised an eyebrow that only I could see, but didn't say anything.

I walked directly to Dana's house, but sleeping over there didn't mean I didn't have my own opportunity for romance. I sent a text to Simon. **Sleep over at Dana's tonight. Wanna come?**

Hell, ya he typed back immediately.

I met Dana at the door with a huge grin. "Guess what?" I shrugged out of my pack, and dumped it on the tiles at the entry.

"What?" she asked warily.

"The guys are coming over. Are your parents going to be home?"

"They're going to Auntie Edie's tonight. We'll have the house to ourselves." She scowled. "I'm making pizza, and I've downloaded some movies for us. Some real tear-jerker chick flicks."

"You're making pizza from scratch?" I shook my head. "You amaze me."

"You're helping. I made the dough this morning, so it is ready to go. Come on."

She dragged me into the kitchen and wrapped a frilly apron around my waist. I looked like a French maid. "Are you serious? What is this supposed to protect my clothes from?"

"I don't think the guys will like my movie choices. I was looking forward to having a girls' night."

I shrugged. "So, they'll download something else. No biggie."

She sighed as the doorbell rang. "You just grate that cheese."

I grated while she went to the door to let Rick and Simon in. I focused on my task, but arms wrapped around me from behind and lips kissed my neck."I love the apron," Simon whispered into my ear. "Very sexy."

I batted him with the grater. "Silly. It's supposed to keep my clothes clean."

"Mmm," he said, nuzzling my neck. "Right."

"Come on, you two," said Dana. "Help make these pizzas.

Rick, here's the dough, do you want to roll it or throw it?"

Rick's eyes twinkled, as he grabbed the dough, "Throw!"

I expected we'd be pulling clumps of dough off the ceiling, but to my surprise, Rick was actually pretty good at tossing the dough into the air, spinning it so that it spread until it was a nice sized disk.

"How did you do that?" I demanded.

He laughed, "Summer job at Luigi's. Tourist girls love watching a handsome young man like myself tossing a pie."

Dana blinked her eyes at him melodramatically and tossed him another ball of dough, "Oh, *signore*," she said it a fake Italian accent, "do it again!"

He kissed the finger-tips of one hand while he spun the dough up with the other one.

Simon pulled a knife out of the block and set it on a cutting board. He reached out to Dana, "Salami if you please? I can slice as well as he can toss."

I imitated Dana's blinking innocence, "Oh, kind sir, do be careful with that big salami!"

Simon threw back his head and howled with laughter. "Oh baby, never fear, there is salami enough for you!"

Dana rolled her eyes, but Rick and I laughed. I tucked my head down so no one would see my blush at the innuendo.

We made a production line, with Rick spreading the sauce, Simon layering the salami, Dana piling on the mushrooms and peppers, and me sprinkling the cheese. We set two pizzas on pizza stones and put them into the oven.

We went into the living room to turn get the movies started, and Simon detoured to the front door. He came back with his pack slung over one shoulder.

"Can you get some glasses, Dana?" he grinned. "I brought

some red wine to go with our Italian dinner. Chianti is required for pizza."

Rick grunted. "It's supposed to be pizza and *beer*."

Simon swung his elbow to whack Rick in the shoulder, "You have no class. If you want to hang out with classy ladies, you have to show a bit of class! So, it is wine, you plebeian, for us, tonight." He pulled a bottle out. The bottom of it was wrapped with a straw basket.

"Ooh! The one they put the candles in!" I giggled. "How romantic!"

He smiled at me. "We have to empty it before we can put candles in it."

Dana set down four wine glasses, and Simon poured for us all. "Let's have a toast to beauty and good cooking!"

Dana and I giggled and sipped the wine. It was nasty. It left a bitter dryness on my tongue.

Simon leaned over and kissed me, his wine flavoured tongue probing for my throat.

The stove timer began to chime, and I started to pull away. Simon laughed and grabbed my butt to pull me closer. I could feel the hardness of him, and it made an unexpected tingle travel up my spine. I leaned into him, and he laughed low in his throat and murmured, "Ah, Last Chance. Do you want me as much as I want you?"

I blushed and looked away.

He gave me a final squeeze and let me go. "Go. Practise being a good wife." He chuckled and patted me on the butt as I walked away.

My heart was pounding as I arrived in the kitchen. *A good wife.*

Dana was pulling the pizzas out of the oven and lining them

up on the racks on the counter.

I took a deep breath. "What can I do?"

"Get the pizza cutter. It's over there." She gestured with her chin.

I rolled it through the pizzas, slicing each into eight pieces. "These look great. Look at that, at least an inch of toppings. You're quite the chef."

She shrugged, "You all helped. It's not hard. Chance..." she broke off and grabbed my arm, "Be careful, eh?"

"I'm being careful! No blood on the pizzas." I winked at her.

"That's not what I mean." She frowned at me. "Be careful with Simon."

"Don't be silly. He loves..." I bit my tongue and rephrased. "He likes me. It's great." He was talking about getting married, after all. I blushed again, at the thought. I could feel him against me. "I'll get Simon's plate," I said. I had to practise being a wife, after all.

~ 12 ~

We passed out the plates and Simon filled the wine glasses again. The movie started. We chewed our excellent pizza and sipped the wine. The more I drank, the better it seemed to taste.

When we finished eating, Rick and Dana curled up together on a recliner and Simon settled me on top of him in another one. I nestled against his chest feeling sleepily content. He wrapped himself around me and kissed my neck as he fondled my breasts. I hoped that Dana and Rick didn't notice.

I cast a furtive glance in their direction, but they were watching the movie, and keeping their eyes averted from us.

Simon burrowed his hand under my shirt and undid my bra in one smooth flick. I gasped, and he chuckled as he cupped his hand around my naked breast. He shifted his hips beneath me, so I could feel him throbbing beneath me.

I sighed happily. My whole body felt electrified.

"I want you, Last Chance," he whispered. "Will you come with me?"

I pondered where he wanted me to go. Back to his town to move in with him? I didn't even know where he was from. We hadn't had any discussions at all. Our joy was more physical than that. It was elemental. I wanted it to last forever. I shifted my body, rubbing against him until he moaned.

"That's it." He rolled onto his hip and pivoted me over the

arm of the chair, he stood up, bent over to scoop me off my feet, and with me giggling helplessly as I thrashed my feet, he carried me over his shoulder into Dana's guest room. He shut the door behind us and tossed me onto the bed. I bounced a bit, and then stood up. He pulled me to him, kissing me until my head was spinning. Then grinning, he reached out for the bottom of my shirt, lifting it smoothly. I raised my arms and was standing in front of him with my undone bra hanging pointlessly in front of me. He slipped it off and leaned in to suck on a nipple. Heat flooded through me, and I wanted him. Badly. I pulled his shirt off and slipped my hand into his jeans. He groaned and undid his zipper. We fell onto the bed, and I thought, *this is really happening. I'm going to lose my virginity to the most handsome guy I've ever met.* Suddenly another thought hit me and I gasped, "Wait! Do you have a condom?"

"Shit. No." He scowled for a minute.

I stared at him, glistening, his penis bobbing like it had a life of its own, nodding, assuring me that it was okay.

"Don't worry. I'll pull out before I come. It'll be all right. You won't get pregnant."

"I don't think..." I started to argue, but then his mouth was on the other nipple, and his hand was on my crotch and then I couldn't think at all.

~ 13 ~

"Chance?" Dana knocked on the bedroom door. "Are you awake?"

"I am now," I mumbled, l looked around trying to figure out where I was, as the night before came rushing back. I turned to say good morning to Simon, but he wasn't there. My heart constricted. "When did the guys leave?"

"After midnight."

"Oh." I fought my way out of tangled blankets and reached for my jeans.

"Are you okay?"

"You can come in," I said, as I pulled on my bra. Dana stepped in. "Why wouldn't I be okay?"

She shrugged. "He didn't hurt you?"

I laughed. "No, of course not." Though, truth be told, I did feel sore. I wasn't going to complain. Simon loved me, and there would be many more nights when we fell into each other's arms and enjoyed each other's bodies. "What's for breakfast?"

"I've got waffle batter proofing. There's fruit, whipped cream, and syrups."

"When did you get to be such a good cook? Are you practising for marrying Rick?"

"Are you crazy? We're in grade ten. Why would you even

think about marriage? We're way too young."

"Living together, then."

She laughed. "I doubt I'll be with Rick that long. How many teen couples end up in long term relationships? Seriously."

"Simon and I will be."

She wrinkled her forehead as she raised her brows.

"I know we will be. He loves me. You'd know if you... Never mind. We will be together."

"Come make waffles."

They were excellent. I kept talking about Simon, how handsome he was, how gorgeous his body was, how great he kissed.

Dana rolled her eyes. "I get it. You're in love."

"Yup," I sighed, folding my arms on the table and resting my head on it. "I'm in love with the most perfect man on the planet."

"I hope you're right."

"What does that mean?"

She shrugged. "I don't know. Something bothers me about him. He's too slick."

"You're just jealous."

"You know I'm not, Chancey. Rick is gorgeous, too. I'm glad you're in love. I just wish I trusted Simon."

I went home feeling kind of sorry for her. She didn't know anything about him. I kept checking my phone for texts. None came from Simon.

I don't know what's wrong! I wrote to Dana. **Do you think he's sick?**

Don't text him, she replied. **You don't want him to think you're needy.**

I am! I need him! But I held off until about midnight.

Finally, I gave in and wrote him a simple, **How was your day?**

He didn't write back.

The next day, I wrote **Miss you.**

He didn't write back.

After three days, I texted to Rick. **What's up with Simon?**

He wrote back, **He's gone home.**

My stomach dropped into my knees and threatened to trip me. **What do you mean home?**

I mean he left. He isn't here anymore.

What's wrong with his phone?

I'm calling you, he wrote, and in a moment my phone rang.

Even though I knew it was Rick, I couldn't help the way my heart leapt in the hope that it was Simon. "Hey."

"Look, Chance. Simon is gone. He isn't coming back, and he won't text you or talk to you."

"Why not?" That didn't make any sense.

"Don't be mad. He said that once he's slept with his current project, he is done with her. He never sleeps with any of them twice."

"Project?" I choked. "What project?"

"You. You were his project. He's done now. He said to tell you you made his holiday really fun."

"Fun?" I said weakly.

"Yeah. He said I should tell you…" He stopped. "Never mind. I probably shouldn't pass that on."

"What? Rick! You need to tell me."

He sighed on the other end of the phone. "Okay fine. He said that you're a great lay, and it he hopes the next guy likes it as much as he did."

"Rick Porter, if you were here, I would slap your face for

that," I growled, fury filling me.

"Don't blame the messenger. When I start sleeping with someone, I am pretty sure I'm going to want keep sleeping with them. He's just weird."

"How many girls has he slept with?" His words were beginning to sink in.

"He said you were his number fifteen for this year."

I choked at that. "He was bragging about it with you?"

"Well, yeah. No offence, Chance. That's just what he talks about. He thought you were great in bed!"

"Such a compliment."

"Exactly." He was serious.

I wanted to puke. "Right. Thanks for telling me. Wish you'd thought about telling before."

"I did. Dana did. You couldn't hear us."

Tears burned in my eyes. Had they tried? I tried to remember. I hadn't heard them if they had. "Yeah. Right," I muttered, trying not to let him hear my tears. "Talk to you later."

I hung up and stared blindly at the TV as I let the tears fall.

So much for my happy ever after.

~ 14 ~

The weeks went by and I did my best to forget about Simon. My parents had never met him, and so I didn't have to answer any questions. Brian asked what had happened to 'that guy you were seeing,' but at my expression he just nodded thoughtfully. He hadn't asked again.

Mom had her period again and spent another week in tears.

I woke in the middle of the night with a turbulent growling in my stomach. I lay there, blinking into the night, absorbing the sensation. Suddenly, the choking urge and I thrust my blankets off me and rushed into the bathroom. I heaved up my dinner, rinsed my mouth, and then brushed my teeth.

"Chancey?" Brian asked, tapping lightly on the bathroom door, "Are you okay?"

"Yeah, I'm fine. My stomach was just upset. I feel all right now." I opened the door and smiled at him. "I'm heading back to bed. Sorry for disturbing you."

"You're sure you're all right?"

I nodded and shut my bedroom door. I heard him rattling around in the kitchen. I rolled over onto my stomach and shifted uncomfortably, my chest hurt, as if my period was coming. I finally had to sleep on my side.

In the morning, I woke to the smell of bacon. I love bacon,

but today it made my stomach churn. I sat up, yawning, and found myself gagging again. I barely made it to the bathroom in time.

"Honey?" said Mom. "Are you throwing up in there?"

"Yeah, I must have the flu."

"Breakfast is ready. Pancakes, eggs, and bacon."

I opened the door and sniffed. "The bacon smells gross."

"You love the smell of bacon," she said, narrowing her eyes.

I wrinkled my nose. "Not today. It makes me want to barf."

Brian came out of their room. Mom looked at him. "Did you hear that?"

He nodded. "She was up last night, too."

"I'm sorry I woke you! I can't help that I have the flu."

"I hope so," Brian said.

Mom tightened her lips.

"What? What's wrong?"

"Nothing, hon. Why don't you go back to bed, if you're not feeling well. I can bring you some pancakes in bed, if you like."

"No, I'll go change and meet you at the table. It's hard eating in bed."

I brushed my teeth. The toothpaste made me gag. I felt strange. Not achey, gross, and really sick like I usually did when I had the flu. My head was fine. It was just my stomach that seemed ridiculously sensitive. And my chest. I pulled back my lips to study my teeth in the mirror. I looked really good, too. I didn't look sick. My hair was shiny and my complexion had cleared up. No zits were in evidence for once.

I pulled on my yoga pants and a t-shirt, humming to myself.

"It's not possible," my mother hissed at Brian, down in the kitchen. "She's a good girl!"

"Of course, it's possible. She had a boyfriend, Megan. All it takes is a boy."

I scowled in the mirror as I headed out into the hall.

"Simon and I broke up, if it's any consolation." I said as I flopped into my chair. Not that we'd ever really been going out, except in my vivid imagination. Turned out he wasn't a very good boyfriend after all, but at least I'd had an adventure.

I sat down at the table and reached out my fork to stab a few pancakes.

"What happened with Simon, Hon?" Mom asked. "Did he do something to make you want to break up with him?"

"Nothing exciting. He had to go back home." They were looking at me with sad puppy eyes, like I was pathetic. "It's okay," I added, trying to look nonchalant. "We decided that a long-distance relationship was not likely to work out, and it was better to break up, that's all."

Brian nodded sagely, "Very mature of you."

I chewed my pancakes and didn't meet their eyes.

"Chancey, I don't want to make any insinuations..." Brian began.

"Brian..." Mom interrupted.

He shrugged, "We have to ask, Megan."

"Ask what?" I said, munching on a mouthful of pancake.

Brian took a deep breath and blurted out, "Is there any chance that you could be suffering from morning sickness?"

"But you only get morning sickness if you're pregnant," I said.

He just looked at me.

I looked over at Mom. She was staring at her plate and

biting her lip.

"I can't be pregnant."

"Because you haven't had sex, right?" said Mom.

My cheeks flamed. "No, because he..." I swallowed and looked out the window. "He pulled out before he..." I swallowed again. "You know."

"Oh, God," said Mom, staring at me.

Brian nodded. "Tell us that you were using a condom."

I blushed again and studied my plate.

"Right. We're making a doctor's appointment for you to take a pregnancy test."

"I really don't think that's necessary," I argued. "I'm not pregnant. I mean, it was only the one time."

"When was your last period?" Mom asked, laying her hand on my arm.

I visualized my calendar and the little check mark that usually went in the first week of the month. I hadn't made one this month and it was almost over. My eyes must have answered the question, because she nodded. "You're having a test."

~ 15 ~

"The doctor phoned," Mom said, as I walked into the kitchen after school. "She wants to see you. I made an appointment for you tomorrow after school. I'll pick you up."

"Did she say why she wants to see me?" Good news or bad news, I meant. I opened the fridge to get the milk.

Mom shook her head. "She didn't."

I poured the milk into my favourite Tweety Bird mug. "It doesn't seem like it'd be worth her time to call me in to tell me that I'm not pregnant, though."

"Yeah. I was thinking the same thing."

I sipped the milk thoughtfully and sighed. What was I going to do?

"Chancey?"

I looked over my mug. Mom's eyes looked funny. Big and shiny, like she was about to cry. They were plaintive eyes, like I used when I wanted them to extend my curfew or buy me a new pair of jeans when I'd used up my allowance. I got a funny feeling in my stomach. "What?"

"If you are pregnant, everything will be fine. You'll stay in school, have the baby, and I'll, I mean, we'll raise her." She stared earnestly at me. "It doesn't have to change anything for you. It will be okay."

I stared at my belly, still flat. It was hard to believe that there could be a person growing in there. It was kind of gross to imagine, actually. Some little alien bean had lodged in my uterus and was going to explode out my privates.

I looked back at her hopeful eyes. "Her?"

"Or him."

"What does Brian say?"

"He's fine with it."

I nodded. Of course, he'd be fine with it. It was the perfect solution for them. Mom got her baby at last. Brian wouldn't have to listen to her crying every month. This was great for her. Was it great for me? "I'm going to get started on my homework," I said, rinsing the glass and setting it into the dishwasher.

I shut the bedroom door and flopped onto my bed.

I'd been an idiot. I had been completely taken in by Simon's good looks and hadn't bothered to get to know the guy under his skin. I had been so keen for a romantic adventure, I'd missed the part about having an actual relationship with someone. I still didn't even know where he lived, let alone how old he was, or what his favourite band was. I had imagined a perfect life with someone who didn't exist.

I knew more about the characters in my silent reading book at school.

Cherie had been right, that warm night when she'd said that he was trouble. Would I have a story to tell her next summer! A month of going out with him, and he'd never even figured out that I was the girl at The Purple Barn.

I had made a terrible mistake, and now I might have to face the consequences of that mistake every day over breakfast. Some little Simon faced person could blink up at me and call me Mom. Me.

The very idea of it made my stomach heave. It heaved again, and I got up and sprinted for the bathroom. This little person was taking after its father already. I was always nauseous around Simon, too.

Mom knocked on the bathroom door. "Chancey? Are you okay?"

"Yeah," I said, flushing the toilet and washing my hands. I brushed my teeth. I could feel her hovering outside the door. "Mom, it's okay. I'm not scraping out my innards with a shaver or anything."

"Chancey!" she squawked. "How can you say such a thing!"

I opened the door and met her eyes. "It was a joke. If I don't joke, I will cry. Would you prefer tears?"

She blinked. Tears were her preferred method of dealing with trauma relating to babies. Maybe she'd never considered that there were other alternatives. She cleared her throat. "Chancey, it will all be fine. You can make whatever decision you need to make, and we'll support you, but know that we love you, and we would love your baby. Our baby. If you want to continue your pregnancy."

I looked into her eyes and understood that a stupid mistake can sometimes bring happiness with it. Simon had given us a weird gift.

It wasn't something I would have wanted, but I had wanted to have sex with him, and I'd been willing to risk it without birth control.

That was dumb.

But.

It would be okay. I had learned some hard lessons in the last couple of months, and I was never going to be able to forget them.

There was definitely enough love in this house to share, though. I leaned over and hugged her tightly. "Thanks, Mom. Let's do this."

LIFE IN LAKETON 4

WILDFIRE!

~ 1 ~

"Come on Zuzu!" I called. "Jump! Jump! Jump!" I ran along the row of dog jumps I'd set up on the dried brown grass of our front yard.

Zuzu, my white standard poodle, ran along behind me, tongue lolling out of her mouth, completely ignoring the jumps. She pulled ahead and stopped short right in front of me, eyes twinkling.

I stumbled, trying not to stop but tumbled over her and collapsed onto the grass, which stuck to my sweaty shirt.

Zuzu wagged her tail and covered me with kisses.

"Oh, Zuzu!" I laughed, rubbing her curly white coat and soft silky ears as I tried to twist away from her tongue. "You win. It's much too hot for this."

My brother Brian pulled up in his pick-up. His red Wildfire Service shirt was filthy, as were his black pants. He looked over to me as he pulled his duffle bag out of the truck. box "That's disgusting, Delia. You're never going to find a boy who wants to kiss you if you let your dog do that."

I was about to argue that I wasn't looking for a boy to kiss, when the screen door opened, and our mom threw her arms wide.

"The prodigal returns!" Our mom threw her arms wide open for a hug. "How's fire fighting?" She beamed at him proudly.

"It's okay. My crew has a day off since our fire is under control. The mop-up crew is going in now."

Mom looked over at me and scowled, "Get off the lawn, young lady! The neighbours will think we're raising a little hooligan instead of a girl! Go put on a dress and come help me with dinner while your brother has a shower." She turned away from me and wrapped an arm around Brian. "Leave your dirty clothes outside the bathroom door and Delia can put them in the laundry for you." She looked up at the sky and glanced over her shoulder at the dark grey clouds gathering over the hills. "Looks like rain at last. You'd better put away those dog things."

I scowled back at her, but she didn't see me, since she'd already followed Brian into the house. That was fine. I was in no rush to put on a stupid dress and do chores my stupid brother was perfectly capable of doing for himself. Why couldn't he take his own clothes down to the laundry room and put them into the washing machine?

Zuzu nudged my elbow. "I know, girl, I know." I could hear my father's serious voice: 'There are pink jobs and blue jobs. Be proud of who you are!' I pulled myself up and went to gather the jumps. As I approached each frame, Zuzu leapt over it like a deer, just to show me she could jump if she felt like it. She glanced back at me with mischief in her eyes as she landed. "You're a brat," I told her, as she bounded over the next jump before I could get to it.

"Your dog doesn't look very smart. That hair cut is ridiculous."

I looked up to see Chris Turlock from school standing at the road.

"She's probably smarter than you. Her hair cut is five hundred years old, created to protect poodles while they're retrieving game from water. It's a hunting hair cut."

Chris just rolled his eyes. "Yeah, right."

I wasn't going to argue with him. Show poodles have super big hair; Zuzu's is much shorter, in the original ancient style. Shaved bare on the back legs to allow for swimming, but with longer hair for protection over the chest, ankle joints and kidneys. I thought it was gorgeous.

Chris watched Zuzu prancing circles around me before he shrugged and came up the sidewalk toward me. "That's Brian's truck, right? Is he home?"

Zuzu stepped between us and stared at him.

He took another step forward.

Zuzu growled. Her whole body was tense

"Whoa there!" He put out his arms, ready to defend himself if she leapt at him. "I'm not going to hurt anybody!"

"How does she know that after all those insults?" I set a hand on my hip and glared at him. I ran my other hand down Zuzu's back. "Good girl."

In the distance there was a rumble of thunder.

Chris took a step back. "I just wanted to see how things are going with Brian."

"He's just gotten back home. He's taking a shower and then he has to have family dinner. You know how my mother is. She needs to gaze adoringly at her favourite child who is risking life and limb to protect the forests. Do you want me to give him a message?"

"Just tell him I'm on the Volunteer Fire Department now. We're training tonight if he wants to come over and give us any tips."

Brian was working for the Wildfire Service this summer. He'd started as a junior firefighter with the Laketon Volunteer

Fire Department when he was fifteen. That gave him training and experience that got him on the Wildfire Service when he was nineteen. It was a dangerous job, but it paid well. I wanted to do it, too, but my parents said it was a 'blue job.'

"I'll tell him." I said, turning away and hoisting the frames onto my shoulder.

"Do you want some help carrying those jumps?"

"Why? Do I look like I need help?"

"Don't be so touchy! I just thought I'd be nice!" Huge drops of rain began spattering on the ground around us in big drops that bounced on the sidewalk pavement and caused puffs of dust where they landed on the dry ground. We hadn't had rain in weeks.

"I'm perfectly capable," I said, hefting three jumps onto my shoulder. "Go to your training. You don't want to be late."

"You know, if you were nicer, you might have a better chance of attracting a boyfriend."

What was it with people thinking I needed a boyfriend? I let out an exasperated sigh and spun on my heels. "Come on, Zuzu."

I side-stepped my way past the raised garden beds that filled the back yard and stacked the jumps against the shed, before I walked back to shut the gate. Zuzu was a good girl, but like most standard poodles, she had a mind of her own. If she felt like visiting Horace the Pug or Daisy the Labrador down the street, she'd be out of the yard. She stood waist high to me and was agile enough to climb any fence, so both our five feet of backyard fence and the gate were really just suggestions. Thankfully, most of the time she just wanted to be with me, and both sufficed.

We didn't have an animal control officer in Laketon, and everyone knew Zuzu belonged to me. Still, I didn't want to see her running loose, where she might get hit by a car or picked up by a tourist who didn't know she had a home.

"Delia!" Mom shouted out the window, "quit fooling with that dog and get in here! We have work to do." She dropped her voice and muttered, "We never should have let you have that puppy."

I smirked. That had been Mom's constant refrain since I'd saved my money from a summer working at Maggie's Shake Shack to buy a purebred standard poodle from performance lines. I wanted a smart dog to train for agility and obedience and I got one. Sometimes I was afraid Zuzu might be training me more than I was training her, but she was my baby and she made me happy.

The rain was pouring down now, so my hair was plastered to my head and Zuzu looked like a wet mop. The longer hair on her head, neck, and back curled up from the moisture.

We stood under the covered deck, and Zuzu shook herself dry, spraying me down. I ruffled her ears and kissed the top of her head. "You're a good girl, Zuzu."

As the backdoor slammed behind us, there was a flash of lightning. Automatically, I began to count under my breath: one thousand, two thousand, three thousand, and then a rumble. The storm wasn't far off.

I walked down the hall and gathered up the pile of clothes Brian had left outside the bathroom, then went downstairs to put them in the washer. When I came back up, Zuzu was turning circles in her basket. She flopped down inelegantly in a tight ball. Brian was in the living room, now wearing his old Laketon High shorts.

Another flash of lightning lit the sky. "I don't like that," he said as the thunder rumbled. "It's so dry out there. Every flash is going to cause a fire that my colleagues are going to have deal

SHAWN L. BIRD

with."

Mom bustled in, "We'll just pray that the rain immediately douses any fire started by lightning," she said. "Delia, I thought I told you to get changed for dinner? Did you put Brian's laundry in?"

"Of course." I bit back the urge to roll my eyes. "Can't you hear the washing machine?"

She tilted her head. "Ah. Good. Thank you. Go get dressed."

There was another flash. Brian opened the front door and sniffed. "Does anyone else smell smoke?"

~ 2 ~

The next morning, there was definitely smoke in the air.

Brian was standing at the back door, looking up to the hill behind our house eating a cereal appetizer, while Mom busily cooked bacon and eggs for his actual breakfast.

"What do you see?" I asked, blinking groggy eyes. I am not a morning person.

He flicked his chin toward the hill. "There's a plume of smoke. Looks like it's up around Hidden Lake Campground."

Zuzu nudged my knee, asking for her breakfast. While I scooped the dry food into Zuzu's bowl, Mom set a heaping plate of bacon, eggs, hash browns, sausages, and toast on the table for Brian.

"Eat up, sweetheart. You need to get lots of food into you, if you're going to have to go back to work right away."

Brian didn't need a second invitation. He sat down and began shovelling the food into his mouth.

"Where's mine?"

"You know where the stove is, young lady. Excuse me, while I get dressed." Mom headed off down the hallway.

I scowled after her. "I hate being a girl in this house." I stomped over to the fridge to get out my own eggs and bacon. There was one egg and two rashers left. "Ah man! This sucks!"

Brian laughed. "Get a plate, she gave me enough for an army. If you're fast, she won't know."

I blinked at the uncharacteristic generosity and brought a plate and cutlery over. He pushed some of his mountain of eggs and a couple of rashers of bacon onto my plate, and settled back into his chair, chewing on his toast.

"Will you have to go back to camp right away?"

He nodded, swallowing. "Probably. I was lucky to get away at all. It's an unexpected break, since those Australian firefighters arrived to help last week." He scooped more eggs into his mouth.

"I'd like to be a firefighter," I said. "It'd be good to feel useful."

Brian started to laugh just as he was swallowing and began choking on his eggs.

I got up and smacked him on his back. "What's so funny!"

He shook his head, wiping tears out his eyes. "You're a girl! Girls don't fight fires."

"That's not true. I know Jan Hollidale's sister was on a fire crew last summer."

Brian rolled his eyes. "The exception doesn't make the rule. Fire fighting is man's work. There is heavy equipment to haul around and it's dangerous in the woods. You can be much more help volunteering to make meals or doing laundry when we come off shift."

"Speaking of laundry," said Mom, suddenly appearing at the table with a stack of folded clothes. I hadn't even noticed her going down to the basement. "Shall I pack this stuff into your duffle for you? I added a few more pairs of briefs and socks, in case you're away from home longer."

'That's great, thanks Mom." He stood and planted a kiss on the top of her head. At over six feet tall, he towered over the rest of us. "Did you hear Delia's latest brainstorm?"

"What's that dear?" She cast a slightly suspicious look over to me.

"She wants to be a firefighter!" he laughed again.

"Don't laugh!" I said at the same time Mom said, "Don't be ridiculous!"

"Mom, girls join fire crew these days! We're not in dark ages anymore."

"Go get dressed, Delia. I am not even going to discuss such nonsense. Imagine what your father would say!"

I went into my bedroom, Zuzu following along behind me. I knew exactly what my father would say. In his most conciliatory voice he'd say, "Why would you want to do a man's job, Delia? You should celebrate that you are a woman and have other gifts." Then he'd look at me solemnly until I apologized for daring to want to do a 'blue job.'

I hated pink jobs and blue jobs! Everyone should know how to cook for themselves and wash their clothes. Why did my family think only women should do those things? Why can't a woman be a plumber or a carpenter? No reason at all. Lots of women did those jobs these days. But not in my family. My family was positively medieval.

"Come here, Zuzu." I flopped on my bed, and she jumped up beside me. Technically, Zuzu wasn't allowed on the furniture, but I was the one who had to wash the sheets, so who should care whether they were dirty except me?

Zuzu let out a contented sigh and dropped her head onto my shoulder.

"I love you, too, girl." I cuddled her warm body and imagined what it'd be like to be old enough to move away and make my own choices. Three more years until graduation and then Zuzu and I were out of here.

My phone pinged and I picked it up. That was another thing my parents disapproved of. They were sure I was going to be lured into all sorts of trouble because I had a cellphone. They even made me keep it in a basket in the kitchen on school nights. Cheers for summer holidays.

The message was from Chris. "Did you tell him?"

I typed back: "Yes." It was a lie, though. I'd completely forgotten once we started dinner preparations. I pulled on shorts and a T-shirt and went to find Brian.

He was scrolling through his own cellphone in the living room.

"Chris told me that he wants to talk to you."

Brian held up the phone. "Yup. He messaged me. You're a bit behind the times."

I shrugged. "Zuzu and I going to do some training. Want to watch?"

"Nah. Not my bag, Delia. I like hunting dogs."

"Poodles are hunting dogs!" I told him for the thousandth time.

"Delia. Just give it up."

"I bet Chris wouldn't care if I joined the Laketon Volunteer Fire Department."

Brian narrowed his eyes, "Are you dating Chris now?"

Another rule at our house was no dating until we were sixteen. I still had a year to go.

"Why does everyone think I want to date? No, I am not dating Chris. I simply know Chris because it's Laketon. I want to join the volunteer fire department."

"No, you don't. You are just saying that because Mom said you couldn't. You're being your typical contrary self, little sister."

"Am not."

"Are, too!" he laughed. And then his beeper went off. The piercing tone filled the house.

Mom appeared at the back door, holding one hand over an ear and the other gripping a basket of vegetables she's just picked from the garden. "Oh, dear! Do you have to go, Brian?"

"Yes. Thanks for breakfast and the clean clothes."

"You're welcome, sweetie," said Mom, setting down a dish of beans glossy with butter. The way she gushed over Brian was seriously nauseating.

"Do you have far to go?" I asked.

"Nope. Just up the hill."

"Oh! That's excellent! Perhaps you'll be home in time for dinner tonight. I'll make a lasagna."

Brian smiled, "That'd be great, Mom, but don't count on it. Looks like this one is going to be trouble. I'll eat with my crew."

"Oh." Mom looked disappointed as she pulled him into a hug.

"I don't mean to scare you," he said over her head, "but this one is close, and the forecast is for wind. It'd be a good idea to prepare a Go Bag with emergency supplies, just in case."

Then he grabbed his duffle bag and headed out the door.

~ 3 ~

Mom watched out the window as Brian drove off down the street. "Your brother is a hero, Delia. I just pray he'll be safe working in those woods!"

"He'll be okay," I said crossing my fingers just in case. "He's got a whole team with him."

Zuzu walked over to the door and rang the bell looped over the handle. I let her out into the yard to do her business. "Do we have an emergency kit ready?"

"No. They're always advertising that every household should prepare for earthquakes and other disasters, but I didn't think they were very likely. Besides, we're good people. Bad things don't happen to good people."

I knew the Old Testament story about the testing of Job, but I didn't argue with her. Mom was pretty set in her ideas. "Should we put something together? Brian would be upset when he'd warned us, if we didn't listen to him." That was psychology. If I said we needed an emergency kit, she wouldn't do it, but Brian was a completely different matter.

"Yes," she said, drawing the word out thoughtfully. "Brian knows about this sort of thing. We should listen to him. I wonder what we should pack?"

"I'm sure there's something on the internet. I'll look," I said, picking up my phone. "Here, Emergency Preparedness Lists from the official government website." I tilted the screen toward her.

Outside, Zuzu started barking.

"What's got into that dog now?" muttered Mom, glancing out the window.

I handed her my phone so she could see the Emergency preparedness list and went out to check on Zuzu.

"Call off your dog!" Chris called from the back gate.

"Zuzu! Back!" I patted my thigh and Zuzu backed up slowly until she was at my side. She stared at Chris with one lip curled and quivering as she growled under her breath. "She doesn't like you very much. What did you do to her?"

"I've never done anything to her!" He opened the gate and came into the back yard.

Zuzu growled but didn't move from her position at my side.

"Good girl," I told her. I rested a hand on her shoulder. She was vibrating with alertness. "Brian's not here. He got paged to go help with the fire at Hidden Lake."

"Yeah, I know. I'm going up there, too."

"They let kids go up to fight forest fires?" I snickered at the expression on his face.

"I'm older than you."

"By five days."

"You should come fight fires, too. The department is looking for more volunteers to help with the Hidden Lake fire. We don't do the front line stuff, but we can do less dangerous stuff to free up the Wildfire Service people for the tough jobs. The department is having a meeting tomorrow. You should come. They'd probably take you."

Ah man. I'd love to join a fire crew. How often as a little kid did I sneak into Brian's room when he was out and put on his volunteer fire uniform, imagining I was a firefighter, too? My mother had freaked out when she caught me one day. I shrugged at Chris. "I can't."

"Why not? I thought you wanted to join/?"

I really didn't want to go into the details of my medieval family attitude, so I just shrugged again. "Did you want something?"

"Uh." Colour rose up his neck and he shuffled his feet in the dirt. "Not really. I just thought I'd let you know I was going up to help."

"Okay."

"And that they're looking for more volunteers, so you should come sign up."

"Okay." Now I was feeling awkward, too. "Well, thanks for telling me. Don't get hurt while you're in the forest."

He nodded. "No. I'll be careful. See you around?"

"Yeah, okay."

He let himself out the gate and I watched until he disappeared around the front of the house. That was weird.

There was a rustle in the bush on the other side of the back fence that abutted the forest. Zuzu's ears perked up.

"Easy girl."

Our house was on the edge of Laketon. A few blocks west of us was the lake. To the south the highway wound along the edge of the lake and took travellers to the nearest city, an hour away. To the north, the highway led deep into the Rocky Mountains. Behind us to the east was forest. Pine and spruce trees soared eighty feet and more. There was a bit of a guard between the fence and the forest, not quite the width of a two-way road. That narrow stretch wouldn't be much defence if a fire roared down the mountain. Our entire street would be devoured.

I went to find Mom's garden hose and the sprinkler head. I connected them and set them in the middle of the raised beds, set to sprinkle the entire back yard. I know it had rained yesterday, but it was already dry in the bed again it was so hot.

Zuzu stood on her hind legs and tried to catch the spray.

I went inside and Zuzu followed behind. I stopped her at the door and ordered her to shake. She all but rolled her eyes at me as she complied, sending water droplets in all directions.

"Mom!" I called. "I put the sprinkler on the back yard, to moisten things up a bit!"

"It's not our day, Delia! We don't want to get a letter from town council!"

"No one is going to complain, Mom. The Smiths and the Lords are both out of town!"

Mom emerged from the basement, another load of laundry in her arms. "That's not the point, Delia. We are law-abiding citizens in this house."

"Yes, ma'am. I'll go turn it off."

"Thank you." She headed off to the bedrooms to put away the laundry.

I pushed the door open and let it shut without going outside. The scent of smoke wafted in.

Zuzu tilted her head in enquiry.

I put my finger to my lips. I opened and shut the door again. Let Mom think I had shut it off. I would rather not have our house burn down.

Mom called out, "Delia, pack your Go Bag. I made a check list. Don't forget you have to make one for the dog, too."

"Her name is Zuzu!"

"I know what its name is, Delia. Pack!"

I took a deep breath and counted to ten before I let it out.

"Let's go get your training bag," I said to Zuzu.

She wagged her tail hopefully.

"No, we're not going to agility class today." I took the shoulder bag I used on Zuzu's training days. It had a couple of tug toys, some snacks, a couple of leashes of different lengths, her cooling vest, a portable water dish, and poop bags. I went to the cupboard for an extra-large zip bag and filled it with several scoops of dog food. That would last for a few days. Zuzu wagged her tail again. She loved going places.

"No, Zuzu. Not today." I hung the bag on a hook at the back door well out of the reach of a treat thieving poodle.

Zuzu rang her bell.

"All right, fine." I opened the door.

Zuzu went onto the deck and sniffed the air. Her whole body stiffened, as she stared into the woods on the other side of the fence, then barking madly she bolted across the wet yard.

"What the heck?" I stepped outside and saw a streak of golden brown moving on the other side of the fence. As Zuzu came toward it, it headed into the woods, Zuzu leapt up onto the frame of one of the raised garden beds, bounded right over the back fence, and sprinted into the forest.

~ 4 ~

"Mom! There's something in the woods! Zuzu just went after it!"

I couldn't believe it. Zuzu loved to race around the agility course, and she was often naughty in class, zooming around the course and not coming when called. At home, though, she usually stayed close to me.

Mom joined me in the yard. We could hear Zuzu barking in the distance. "What is it chasing?"

"I'm not sure. It was low and brown."

"Deer?"

"I don't think so, it didn't really move like a deer."

"Huh." She moved to the fence, which was almost over her head. "She just jumped over the fence?"

I pointed to the raised bed. "She used that as a springboard and just bounded right over! I am going to have to go in the woods to find her."

"It's a dog, Delia. It knows how to find its way home. That's what animals do."

"But there's a forest fire up there! Who knows what could be lurking in the woods!"

"You know very well what's lurking. Deer. Bears. Coyotes. Elk. Cougars. Wolves."

My mouth was suddenly dry. Poodles are smart, and Zuzu looked like a big dog standing at my hip, but she only weighed forty-five pounds. She'd be no match for a wolf or a cougar. "I have to go find her."

"How? Get your hiking boots on and wander aimlessly through the forest? Don't be ridiculous, Delia. It's a dog. It'll come back on its own." She walked back to the house. "Come in and finish packing your Go Bag. You don't want Brian to be disappointed in you."

I stood at the fence staring into the forest where Zuzu had vanished. I didn't care at all about disappointing my brother. I cared about my best friend.

Specks of something were falling from the sky. I looked at the back of my arm where a thin line of grey as long as a fingernail had landed. I touched it, and it dissolved into powder. Ashen evergreen needles.

Brian was the least of my concern. I needed to get Zuzu back home before she was a pile of ash.

"Delia!" Mom shouted out the kitchen window.

I whistled the three short blasts that were my signal when Zuzu was supposed to come right away. I listened, hoping to hear branches rustling or barking coming closer. Branches were moving. Wind had picked up and the tops of the trees were bending and dancing in the acrid air. Nothing sounded like it was moving through the undergrowth, though.

I heard a snorting, snuffling bark down the street. That was Horace the pug, down the block. Horace was safely home in his yard where a dog belongs. Zuzu, what were you thinking! I whistled again, but not even Horace answered this time.

The trees waved as the wind increased.

I needed an action plan. Maybe Mom was right, maybe Zuzu

would come back on her own, but maybe something was luring her deeper into the forest and was planning to attack her. Zuzu was fast and she had great stamina, but she wasn't a fighter, despite all the stuffed animals she'd eviscerated in growling, shaking, fervour.

I went into the kitchen just in time to hear a buzz as my phone that I'd left on the counter began to vibrate. A musical tone alerted me to a text message. It was from Chris.

"Did you see the news? All of Laketon is on Evacuation Alert."

"What? Why?"

"Hidden Lake Fire is moving in toward town, fast. Go sign up on the Emergency Alert app so you always hear the latest news."

"I will. Thanks!" I set down my phone, heart pounding. "Mom!" I called out. "Laketon is on Evacuation Alert! The fire is moving this way!"

"What?" Mom appeared from the hall where the bedrooms were. "Who told you? Is this just hearsay?"

"Chris texted me. He's with the Laketon Volunteer Fire Department. He knows what's going on."

Mom pursed her lips like she wanted to argue with Chris or the fire or more likely me.

"Let's check the official emergency website," I suggested. "Chris said they also have an alert app; all the official information will be there."

Mom went to the computer and typed into the search engine so slowly I wanted to shove her out of the way to do it myself. "Oh." She said when the page came up. "It's true. It's not all of Laketon, just the southwest half. But we're on alert all right. Oh dear." She took a deep breath. "Your brother was right, wasn't he? I'll move the Go Bags into the car. Have you got yours packed?"

"Not yet. I got Zuzu's ready, though." The thought of Zuzu out in the woods with a fire raging toward her made me cold all over.

"I'll get some water and food packed. You go do your Go Bag."

I stood at the door to my bedroom and looked around. I didn't know quite where to begin. What do you take when you might never see whatever you leave behind? I pulled my backpack out from under my bed where I'd stashed it after school ended in June. I dumped out the binders and pens.

What to bring?

Underwear. I would definitely need underwear. I stuffed seven pairs and a couple of bras into the bottom of the pack. Shorts. Pants. A few T-shirts. A jacket. A hat. Jeans. I went into the bathroom and dug around for a new toothbrush and the travel toothpaste. I grabbed chargers and my laptop bag. Then I went into Brian's room and rummaged in his closet until I found the boots he'd worn as a junior firefighter. With a pair of thick socks, they'd be fine for me.

The pack was full. My heart was heavy.

I took the pack into the kitchen, and then took the bag I'd prepared for Zuzu down from its hook. I took both bags to the garage where Mom was arranging things into the trunk.

"Do you have our passports and important papers, like marriage and birth certificates?"

She nodded.

"What about mortgage information and insurance?"

"Not yet. Good idea. We'd definitely need our insurance information if the house burnt down."

I stared into the trunk. "This is scary."

Mom reached out and gave me a hug. She wasn't a particularly huggy person, but we clung together in the garage. "It'll be okay, Delia. You'll see. If we need to, we'll get somewhere safe."

But would Zuzu?

Once the car was packed up, we had nothing to do but twiddle our thumbs and nervously check social media for updates.

We could hear the whir of the planes as they came low, skimming the lake to fill their pontoons with water, to release over the fire. A helicopter rotors thumped as it came low enough to fill its bucket, and then head up the mountain to dump it on the fire.

I wanted to walk down the block to sit on the beach and watch, to get the feeling that I was doing something if only just to observe the firefighters' hard work, but I was afraid of being away from home if the Evacuation Order came.

My first priority was Zuzu, though. I needed to find her. I opened up my laptop and made a poster that said "ZUZU IS MISSING!" Looking through my pictures for a perfect one of her made me cry. I had hundreds of pictures of her. Pictures at agility trials as she jumped over bars, leapt through a tire, burst out of a tunnel climbed the A-frame or raced along the raised dog run. In each photo her eyes were bright with fun and determination. She loved playing in agility. There were also lots of shots of her sleeping in cute positions or posing with new hair cuts. Professional standard poodle grooming is really expensive, so I bathe and clip Zuzu myself each month myself. Sometimes I intentionally give her a weird hair cut, but lots of the time, they're weird because I screwed up. That's okay. I'm learning. Besides, Zuzu doesn't care. She swaggers like a top model whatever she looks like.

When people see us out walking and ask who does her grooming, they ask if I'll do their dogs, too. So I have a little side business, bathing and shaving down dogs that the owners don't brush properly because when they got them, someone told them they have low maintenance coats. It gives me a few hundred extra dollars each month.

I picked a photo of Zuzu, freshly groomed, her coat gleaming white as she stood, looking alert and happy. I added my cellphone number for contact on a series of tear-offs at the bottom and sent twenty copies to the printer. Then I had to cut all the tear-off slits with the phone number.

"Mom! I'm going out! I'm going to put up some posters of Zuzu."

"Take your phone!" she called back.

I hopped on my bike with a bag full of posters in the little basket I had on the handlebars.

"Nice dog," said a lady as she watched me staple a poster on a telephone poll down the block.

"Thanks."

"What happened? Did someone steal her? I had a friend whose dog was taken by those ladies who cruise through neighbourhoods luring dogs to lure they take out of province to sell as bait dogs to dog fighting rings."

I blanched. "Oh! That's awful! Did she get the dog back?"

"Yeah. Someone had spotted the truck and taken the license plate. The police stopped it and seized the four dogs in the back. But they got off eventually with a fine. Not high enough to stop them from doing it again. I always worry when I see a missing dog poster."

I shuddered, "Zuzu wasn't taken. She spotted an animal in the woods behind our house and jumped our fence."

The lady shook her head. "That's rough. Toward the fire?"

I nodded, blinking back tears.

"I hope you find her. I'll keep my eyes out and spread the word."

I thanked her and rode off.

I was putting my last poster up on the bulletin board at the strip mall when my friend Sara came up on her skateboard.

She read the poster. "Zuzu is lost? That's horrible!"

"She's in the forest. I am afraid she's going to be eaten by a bear or something."

Sara shook her head, "No way. Zuzu is fast. She'd outrun any bear. She'll be okay. And she loves you. You know she wouldn't stay away from you for long. When did she disappear?"

"Last night." I checked my phone. "She's been gone twelve hours." Twelve hours was a long time in the woods. Anything could have attacked her.

"You guys are on Alert, eh?" Sara said.

I nodded.

"It's so scary. Our part of town isn't on alert, but my mom said, 'better safe than sorry' and made us pack Go Bags, too. Kieran was really grumpy about it."

"We've got the car packed, ready if we have to go. I've got Zuzu's stuff, but no Zuzu. What happens if we are ordered out, and she's not back yet?" The thought made me sick to my stomach.

"Where will you go if you have to leave? There are no hotels available because of the tourists who've stayed to finish their holiday."

"I don't know. Dad's out of town visiting my grandparents and Brian's up fighting the fire, so it's just Mom and me. I don't know what she'll want to do." I brushed tears out of my eyes imagining the fight that was bound to happen. "I don't want to leave until I've got Zuzu, but how will that work?"

"Come stay with us. I've got an extra bed in my room. It'll be like a sleep over. I know my mom won't mind."

"That would be great, actually. I'll ask Mom and see what she says. She'll probably want to talk to your mom and makes sure it's okay."

At that moment, a blaring alarm blasted from my pocket, making up both jump.

"What's that?" Sara said, as I pulled my vibrating phone from my pocket.

"Emergency app." My heart was pounding in my throat as I read the message. "All of Laketon is on evacuation alert now, and my half of town is ordered to evacuate the area immediately."

~ 6 ~

I raced back home where Mom was waiting in the driveway, pacing back and forth. "Where have you been!" she called out, as soon as she spotted me coming down the road.

"I told you I was putting up posters about Zuzu."

She just scowled. "We're on evacuation order, Delia!"

"I know. That's why I came home. I got the message, too."

"I didn't know when you'd be back."

"I had my phone. Why didn't you text if you wanted to know where I was?"

Mom pinched her mouth, because she didn't want to admit I was right.

I held up the phone, showing the flashing red alert message. "It says we have to register at the Community Centre on the other side of town and let them know our plans."

She nodded tersely.

"Hey, can I put my bike on the rack and bring it with me? It'd be good to have transportation."

"I thought we'd just go straight to your grandparents in Victoria. The sooner we get to a ferry the better."

I stood beside my bike. "You can go to Victoria, but I'm not. I need to stay here to look for Zuzu.

"Delia."

"Mom." I clipped the bike rack onto the back of the car and attached my bike into it before climbing into the passenger seat.

"Young lady, this is more important than a dog."

"Zuzu is my dog. You told me that a dog was a serious responsibility and if I insisted on getting a dog, I would be the one who had to keep her safe and healthy. Remember?"

Mom nodded; eyes narrowed. "Yes, but…"

"I promised to look after her the best I can until she dies. So I'm going to find her."

"It ran into a forest fire, Delia. It's probably already dead."

A red-hot fury raced through me as we pulled into the Community Centre parking lot. It was full of people milling around nervously.

A volunteer in a safety vest and carrying a clip board came over. "Hi Mary-Beth. Hello Delia. Registration is just through those doors."

Ashes were falling from the sky, like sparse snowflakes.

"Thank you, Carol!" Mom called with a fake smile. She turned back to me. "And where do you think you're going to stay if I were to leave you behind?"

"Sara invited me to stay with them. Their house is just on alert."

Mom gave a snorting noise as she found the line that coincided with our street address. "Just on alert. Fifteen minutes ago we were 'just on alert' and now we're registering with emergency services while we abandon our home!"

"Please, Mom?" I stared at her with all my desperation in my eyes. "I need to find Zuzu."

She rolled her eyes and muttered, "I have to talk to Meghan and make sure it's okay."

"Thank you!" I threw my arms around her.

"Oh look! She's one of the registration volunteers. You can ask her now."

When we got to the front on the line, Mom smiled wanly at Sara's mom.

"Hello Mary-Beth. Scary times, eh?" said Mrs. Smith.

"Hi Meghan. Yes. Incredibly scary."

Mrs. Smith flipped through some papers until she found the one she wanted. "Address?"

Mom repeated it.

"Perfect." She ticked a line on the paper. "How many in the household?"

"Four. But only two to register."

"Oh. You'd better give me the details."

"Robert, my husband is out of town right now. Our son Brian is fighting the fire. He's working with the Wildfire Service this summer. So it's just Delia and me."

"Good." Mrs. Smith winked at Delia. "What are your evacuation plans?"

"I will go to Victoria. That's where Robert is. Delia has lost her dog and doesn't want to leave until it's found. She says Sara invited her to stay at your house?"

Sara's mom smiled. "Yes. She mentioned that. It's absolutely fine with me. Sara has a room with two beds in the basement where it's lovely and cool. No air conditioning in the rest of the house, I'm afraid."

"That's okay," I said quickly. "Thanks so much Mrs. Smith. I really appreciate it."

"Not a problem. All right, I just need contact phone numbers for you both?"

She wrote our cell phone numbers on the form and then took a piece of scrap paper and wrote a number on it. "That's everything then. Mary-Beth, if the rest of town is evacuated, we will go to Calgary where we have some family. Here's my number." She slid the paper across the table. "We'll take Delia and Zuzu," she smiled at me, "it won't be a problem. Don't worry."

"Thank you. That's very kind. I am sorry she's being such a bother."

"No bother." She glanced past us and nodded to whoever was behind us in the line.

"Thanks again," Mom said as we left the line and walked back to the car.

"I am not happy with this, Delia."

"I know. I'm sorry. I just can't leave Zuzu!"

"Come on, I'll drive you over to Sara's house."

Sara was at their front door and waved as we pulled up. "Yay!" she called, as I opened the car door. "I'm so glad you're staying."

"It was kind of you to invite her," Mom said as she glanced at her watch. "You be sure to behave, Delia."

"I always behave!"

"You, too, Sara," she added.

Sara blushed. "I'll do my best, Mrs. [Delia's last name]" she said as she took my bag.

I lifted the bike off the rack. "I should keep the bike rack, in case we need to evacuate from here, too."

Mom just sighed as I undid the straps and clips, but before I was ready, she reached for my shoulder and pulled me into a hug. "You be careful! Don't do anything stupid while you're looking for that dog. I love you."

"I love you, too. Mom. Say hi to dad and Grandma and Grandpa."

She nodded, sniffing and blinking. She climbed back into the car, waving as she pulled out of the driveway. She had a five-hour drive to the ferry.

It was weird being left.

Sara threw an arm around my shoulder. Come on. Leave the bike and rack there in the corner."

We walked into the house. It was hot inside, but the air was considerably fresher than it was outside. I hadn't really noticed the smoke as we were in it, but now we were inside I started to cough.

"Hi, Delia," said Sara's brother Kieran as we walked past the living room where he was playing some game on his phone.

I nodded a greeting. We were still on the basement stairs when my phone rang. I didn't recognize the number.

"Hi." said a deep male voice. "Are you the one that lost the big poodle?"

My breath caught. "Yes! Have you seen her? Do you have her? Is she all right?"

"I don't have her, sorry."

"Oh." My heart plummeted into my belly.

"But I think I've seen her. I am on the fire crew. I was driving out when I saw a flash of white in the trees. At first, I thought it was a deer, but as I was driving out, I was thinking it was too small and light coloured. I just saw your poster. It makes sense that it was your dog."

"That's great! Can you tell me exactly where?" I could ride my bike up the forest road with one of Zuzu's leashes. She could run out. Or maybe this guy would drive me up.

"About the seven-kilometre marker, I'd say."

"Could you take me up there?"

"Sorry. You can't go up there right now. They are moving

the crews because the fire leapt the first line. It's not safe for you. I just wanted you to know that the dog is still out there."

"Yes. All right. Thank you for calling."

If it wasn't safe for me in the woods, it sure wasn't safe for Zuzu.

~ 7 ~

The next afternoon the sky was brown with acrid smoke that burned the eyes and throat. Sara, Kieran and I were sitting in their basement watching a DVD when my phone pinged a text message.

Chris had written, "Where are you?"

"At Sara and Kieran's," I typed back.

"I'm off for today. Wanna go to Maggie's?"

"Why are you off? What's happening with the fire?"

"It's still moving, but we're building a new firebreak and the water bombers are keeping it back while we do. Wanna meet me for a shake?"

"Can I bring S and K?"

There was a long pause before he replied, "Sure."

I looked up from the phone and asked, "You guys want to go to Maggie's? Chris is going and invited us along."

Kieran snorted. "Chris invited me? Right. Sure he did."

Sara laughed, "You're a necessary evil, dear brother. Chris has a thing for Delia. He's been after her for ages."

"He has not!" I yelped.

She just snickered and shook her head. "You keep telling yourself that."

"We are just friends. Barely friends!" narrowing my brows

at her. "Zuzu hates him."

"Really? Did he have anything to do with her disappearance?"

"No, she leapt that fence of her own volition, and it definitely wasn't Chris who taunted her from the woods." I looked back at the phone. Chris had texted me a question mark. "Shall we go?"

Sara stood up, "Of course. Come on, brother mine. Come watch Chris attempt to capture Delia's heart."

"Should be good for a laugh," he said.

"You two both be nice," I glared at them. "Or none of us will go."

Kieran just grinned. "Tell him we'll meet him there in ten minutes. We should probably put on masks, though. The smoke is really thick out there."

We walked up Larch Street to Maggie's Shake Shack in our masks.

"Do you still work at Maggie's, Delia?" asked Kieran.

"Sometimes. I was full-time last summer, but I just wanted a few hours this year. They mostly call me when someone doesn't show up. I have been doing mobile dog grooming, too."

"Oh right! I heard someone talking about that in the Bargain store once. You go to their house?"

I nodded, "Yeah. I had to get this expensive equipment so I can groom Zuzu, so I just added people when they asked. I have a bag of stuff I put in the basket of my bike and do the grooming at their house. People pay in cash." I shrugged.

"How much do people pay to have their dog groomed?"

I shrugged again, "Depends. Little dogs I charge fifty bucks for bath, dry, trim."

"How long does it take?"

"An hour or two. The better I know the dog the faster it is. I don't do anything fancy."

"Wow." Kieran stared at me. "You average thirty-five bucks an hour."

Sara punched him in the arm. "You're being rude."

"Why? I'm impressed. The guys working at the dock are happy to make eighteen."

"I would never have learnt if not for Zuzu." I missed her so much. Thinking about her lost in the woods made my stomach twist into writhing knots.

When we arrived at Maggie's, Chris was sitting at a picnic table out front. He greeted me and Sara but ignored Kieran.

Kieran winked at me behind his back as we went inside to order.

Kieran had rum raisin milkshake. Sara had double chocolate sundae. I ordered a triple dipped cone. Chris had a vanilla shake.

I sat down at the picnic table Chris had been at. Kieran sat beside me, grinning at Chris's scowl. Sara sat on the other side across from Kieran, so Chris sat facing me.

"Delia," said Kieran in a deliberately casual tone, "what kind of person traditionally orders a vanilla milkshake? Are they as boring as I think they'd be?"

Sara kicked his shin under the table, but so obviously that we could all tell she was doing it.

Chris's neck was turning red.

"Don't be a jerk, Kieran." I turned my back to him and asked Chris, "What's happening with the fire? Is it getting closer?"

Chris shrugged. The water bombers are keeping it back and trying to push it up the mountain away from town.

Sara smiled at him, "What is your crew doing?"

"We're helping with the firebreak above the point at the moment. The Wildfire Service has heavy equipment clearing a strip of land and the Laketon Fire Department is helping to clear flammable debris out of it."

"Sounds exhausting," Sara said.

Chris nodded, "Yeah. Dirty, hot, and tiring. But it might save Laketon. So I'm glad to be out there doing it." He looked meaningfully over to Kieran, who developed a slow smirk, but didn't respond to the implied insult.

"A firefighter told me he thought he saw Zuzu up on the forestry service road yesterday."

"It's so weird she'd go into the forest when most animals are running away from the fires."

Kieran snickered. "Seriously? You didn't see all the posters? What kind of hopeful boyfriend are you?"

Chris's neck got even brighter red, but he turned from Kieran and looked earnestly at me. "What happened?"

"She saw something in the forest, jumped our fence, and chased after it. She's been gone two days now."

"I didn't know. I'm sorry."

His eyes didn't look sorry. He looked like he was glad the demon spawn who defended me wasn't there to stand between us anymore.

Just then, a truck full of fire fighters pulled up. They were still in the gear with hard hats and filthy uniforms. Ash was smeared on their faces.

"Hey, Chris," one said as he went by. "Is this the girl?"

Chris's colour rose from his neck into his face. He sputtered, "Ah, these are friends from school." He pointed at us as he told our names.

"Delia?" said one. "Are you the one on all the lost poodle posters?"

"Yes. Have you seen her? A firefighter in a truck saw her

near a road yesterday."

"I didn't see her myself, but one of the pilots was saying this morning that he thought he saw a skinny white dog run into sight, just as he was making a water drop."

"A water drop." I stared at him as I visualized that. "Wait. Dropping water ON THE FIRE?" My voice had risen several pitches. What was Zuzu doing that near the fire?

~ 8 ~

The firefighters went inside to get their ice cream and I sat eating my double dip cone and pondering.

"Are you okay?" Chris asked.

"Where are the fire lines, now?"

"Pardon?"

"The fire lines. Do you know if Zuzu has crossed the fire line and gone closer to the fires? That doesn't make any sense. Animals know to instinctively move away from fires, don't they. Zuzu isn't stupid."

"I have only seen animals coming out of the fire zone."

"Why would Zuzu go in?" I muttered to myself.

"Do you think she could be protecting something," asked Sara. "Were poodles bred as livestock guardian dogs or herders?"

"No, they're water retrievers. They were meant to go after ducks and geese shot by hunters, you know, the ones that fall into lakes and ponds. Though Zuzu does like to herd children and will guard our yard against neighbourhood cats."

Sara laughed.

Chris snorted, "Zuzu thinks she's a protection dog. You should see how she snarls when I come near Delia."

"That's just good sense. She reads danger," Kieran drawled with a smirk to me.

Chris sputtered and would have argued, but Kieran lifted a placating hand. "No, no. I'm just joking. Don't get yourself in a knot."

He looked at me thoughtfully, "What do you think made her jump out of the yard? Could she have been trying to protect you from something? There are a lot of predators in the forests."

There was flurry of activity around us as the fire crew found seats around a nearby picnic table some of them with more than one dessert. One had a milk shake, a banana split, and a brownie sundae in front of him and was brandishing a spoon with gusto.

"Are the animals leaving the woods? Have we seen more wildlife in town?" Sara asked glancing at each of us in turn.

I shrugged. "I haven't heard anyone say anything. I haven't seen anything. Have any of you?"

The others shook their heads.

It wasn't uncommon for deer, elk, or bears to wander through town. We were surrounded by forest. We had lots of rules about putting out our garbage, to avoid drawing bears into town on pick-up days.

One of the firefighters leaned over. "There are definitely more animals moving toward town and the shore of the lake. I was in the helicopter and saw a family of bears coming across the beach access along the highway yesterday and there are lots of deer hovering in beach front property. Now that the highway is closed, it's a bit of a wildlife corridor. There are lots of deer on the move. I suspect most animals try to get through town at night. Certainly the wildcats and deer are most active at dawn and dusk."

I fought the lump that rose in my throat at his news.

"Why do you ask?" he added.

"Her dog is lost," said Kieran, glancing at my face and reading my distress. "She went into the woods Sunday night chasing after something."

"Oh, I'm sorry to hear that," said the fire fighter. "Just one day is a long time to be out in the woods during a forest fire."

He looked so glum, I knew he thought there was no hope that Zuzu was all right, and I burst into tears.

Kieran put an arm around my shoulder. "Shh. It'll be all right. Zuzu will come back. You'll see."

I closed my eyes and leaned into him. Across the table, I heard Chris harrumph.

This wasn't good. I couldn't just wait here like a ball of goo, waiting to hear Zuzu's fate, or worse, having to look for her charred remains after the fire was out. I sat up straighter. I smiled my thanks at Kieran, who offered a gentle smile.

"Chris," I said, my voice steely with determination. "Who do I talk to about joining the fire department?"

Beside us, the fire crew whooped, and one patted me on the back. "That's the attitude, missy!"

Missy.

Jerk.

"I can take you over to the hall right now. The captain is bound to be there. He's really busy coordinating everyone. I'm sure he'd be glad to have you."

Kieran leaned over, his shoulder nudging mine. "Are you sure about this? It's dangerous to fight fires."

I nodded.

Sara took my hand and gave it a squeeze. "I think it's a good idea. You'll be able to talk to more people and see if there are more sightings. The more people looking for Zuzu, the better her chances of being found." She stood up to put her sundae dish into the garbage can. "I'll walk you over, too. Coming Kieran?"

Chris gave Kieran a look of hatred that would have made me

laugh under less stressful conditions. I didn't acknowledge I'd seen anything, put my cone wrapper into the garbage, and after dabbing my mouth, tossed my serviette after it.

Kieran stood as well, lobbing his milkshake cup over their heads. It plopped neatly into the garbage. He winked at me. "I have some stuff to do, so I'll head back home." He looked at Sara and added, "See you both by six o'clock for dinner."

Sara glanced at her phone to confirm the time and nodded. "Sounds good. We'll be there."

The three of us started walking toward the fire house by the highway junction. With Sara on my left and Chris on my right, I felt like I had my own honour guard.

If I could get onto a fire crew, I could go into the woods, and I could find Zuzu.

At them meeting, they gave us paperwork to fill out and we got to practice with some of the tools. With all my sizes recorded, they would have official fire safe uniform for tomorrow. I just needed to have my own boots. I was thankful I'd thought to take Brian's old ones.

I took my papers off to the bathroom, and sitting on the toilet, I forged my parents' signatures. What they didn't know wouldn't hurt them.

I couldn't just sit around waiting for bad news. There'd be two sightings. I knew where to look. I had to get out there and rescue Zuzu from whatever situation she'd got herself into. I would find Zuzu, I would. Zuzu had to be okay. She just had to be.

What would I do if I lost the only thing in the world who loved me unconditionally?

~ 9 ~

Thursday night we'd stayed up late and walked down to the lake shore. Along with a lot of Laketon families, we sat silently on the benches, logs, and rocks watching the vivid swaths of red and orange throbbing like luminous lava in the hills. The stars were gone. The moon glowed an ominous red. We coughed at the acrid bite of the smoke, but stayed anyway, mesmerized by the sight of the menace in the hills above town. We sat vigil, sending our thoughts or prayers to the sky to whatever deity might protect our homes and the firefighters.

The next morning the smoke was so thick we could see wisps floating in the road in front of the house. The world appeared in soft focus. Ash covered everything. There were little flecks of grey, like nail clippings on the deck chairs. These ashen evergreen needles dissolved to powder when we brushed them off.

The water bombing planes and helicopters were out.

"It's like living in Armageddon," Sara said, sipping her iced coffee as we sat on their back deck and looked at the billows of smoke in the hill. The air had a brown tinge. It was like looking at sepia toned photos.

"It's getting closer isn't it?" I whispered to Sara. "My neighbourhood is going to be the first to burn."

"Don't say that. Look how hard the crews are working! Remember what Fire Chief Parker said about the retardant and the fire breaks? I think it will work."

Kieran stepped onto the deck with his hands curled around his own coffee. "You only think it will work because you're an optimist. Delia is right to be concerned. It's not looking good."

Sara grunted. She'd picked up her phone and was scrolling. "The forecast says the wind direction is going to change, and the fire is going to be pushed over the mountain away from town," she stuck out her tongue at Kieran, "so there!"

"I'm going to text Brian and see if he knows anything more," I said. What good was having a brother on the fire line if I couldn't wheedle him for information? I sent off a message and waited.

"Is he in cell range? They might not be able to connect up in the hill if any of the cell towers have burnt down."

Sara scowled at him. "Why must you be so negative!"

"I'm just being realistic! Delia needs a rational advisor at a time like this." He glanced over to me. "Let's go in. This smoke is just gross. I'll make you both another ice coffee."

"Thanks," I said, "that'd be nice." I pushed past him and set my cup on the kitchen counter. Then I went into the living room and collapsed on the couch. Movement from the corner of my eye made me do a double take. "Sara! Come here!"

Sara ran over and joined me at the window. "Oh! Gosh!"

"What is it? called Kieran from the kitchen.

"You won't believe it," Sara said, "come see!"

Kieran came in with his hands wrapped in a dish towel. "Oh!"

The three of us sat kneeling on the couch, arms on the windowsill and watched as three deer stole green apples from a neighbour's tree.

Several rabbits were sitting on various neighbour's lawns, munching.

A large black bear and two cubs almost the same size were strolling down the street.

The deer's ears flicked nervously, but they kept eating until the bears stepped onto the lawn. Then the deer bounded down the road, and the bears all stood on their haunches to investigate the tree.

A tone announced a text message. Brian had replied, "Fire is moving. I'm busy."

Another tone announced a message from my mom. "How are you?"

I got off the couch and wandered into the kitchen. "Everything's fine," I wrote back. Sara's family are kind hosts. How are you and dad?" I definitely wasn't going to tell them I was volunteering with the Fire Department, or that the fire was moving closer to the town. They worried enough as it was.

"We're fine. Dad says hello. Have you heard from Brian?"

"Yes. He's busy working. Are Grandma and Grandpa doing okay? Is she out of the hospital now?"

That got her talking. For ten minutes she discussed Grandma's operation and the renovations needed for her house and all the things they were doing to help. There was a crash and she said, "Oh no! The dishes! Talk to you later."

I waited for a 'Love you!' but the phone went silent. I shouldn't have been in the least surprised.

"Holy!" Kieran whispered. "This is bizarre!"

Sara just gasped.

I went back to the window and stared at the massive cougar walking down the road.

"It's like living in a bloody zoo!" Kieran said.

"We shouldn't be surprised. Their home is burning. Where else are they going to go?"

"Isn't it funny," I said, watching the incredible grace of the big cat's muscles rippling, "that yesterday we hadn't noticed any wildlife in town, and today we see this?" The cat was huge.

We watched as it lowered its head and crouched, staring. All that moved was its flicking tail.

"Uh oh," said Kieran. "I think one of those rabbits is about to be dinner."

"I can't look!" said Sara turning as the cougar pounced.

Another tone on my phone made me look away, too.

"Got it!" said Kieran. He hooted with laughter, "Look at the rest of them go!" At least six rabbits were sprinting in all directions.

I glanced down at my phone. Chris had written, "Situation briefing and crew assignments. Fire Hall at nine o'clock. See you there?"

I sent back a thumb's up icon.

I flipped through messages I'd missed, and there was the one from the fire dispatch about the meeting. I looked at the time. I had about forty-five minutes to get to the hall. It was only a ten-minute bike ride, so I had time to grab something to eat.

"I've got a meeting. What's for breakfast?"

Kieran and Sara joined me in a production line to make toast, bacon, eggs, and fresh fruit. I made myself a scrambled egg and bacon toasted sandwich to eat there and put an orange in my pocket for a snack later. "See you guys, later," I said heading toward the door.

"Wait," said Kieran. "You shouldn't go by yourself when there are bears and cougars strolling the streets."

"I am pretty fast on my bike, though."

"Both a bear and a cougar can outrun your bike," Kieran said thoughtfully. "I'll ride with you; I can distract anything wanting to attack you."

"I'll come, too. I have my longboard," Sara added. "And I'll bring the bear spray cannister."

~ 10 ~

The trip to the Fire Hall was relatively uneventful. We saw deer down one side street. A bear in the distance down another, but the cougar didn't stalk us (I don't think!) and being on wheels means we were early for the meeting.

Chief Parker came over to us, eyeing Kieran and Sara. "New recruits?"

"No, we were just escorting Delia to ensure she got here safely. There's a lot of wildlife in town."

The chief nodded. "Yes, I've been hearing lots of reports. You saw a bear?"

"Deer, bear, and we saw a cougar nab a rabbit this morning," Kieran explained.

"Really? I hadn't heard any reports about a cougar come into town. Where did you see it? I'll send a report to the Fish and Wildlife Service. I would hate one to get comfortable here. It'd have to be killed. They're too dangerous for little kids and pets."

Pets like Zuzu.

"Sir," I said, "have there been any reports of a dog in the fire zone?"

"Ah, you're the one with the missing standard poodle?"

I nodded.

He looked around the room, "Davis! Come talk to Delia!"

A tall guy, maybe late twenties or early thirties came over. Neither his uniform nor his hands were particularly clean. He had clearly been fighting the fires recently. "Yeah, Chief?"

"Weren't you the one in the helicopter early this morning? Did you see something?"

"Yeah, I thought it was a sheep at first. Then I figured it was one of those curly dogs. Doodle?"

I bristled a bit. "If it was Zuzu, she's got a pedigree full of champions. She's not a mutt like a doodle."

Davis shrugged. "Whatever. Whitish dog. Can't tell more from the air."

"Yeah, sorry." I muttered. "Where was she?"

"Up the forestry service road, in the area where we are going to be starting mop-up today, actually."

"Really?" That was the best news I'd had in days.

"There's a grizzly up that way, too. We have seen it a couple of times moving through the area."

"Oh." That was worse news.

I spotted Chris as he came into the hall.

He waved, then checked his enthusiasm and strolled over to us. "What's up?" he said, all chill.

Ignoring the idea of a grizzly near town, I flashed a grin at him that made him step back. "Davis spotted Zuzu! We're going to be working in the same area today! Maybe we'll see her!" I turned to the chief. "When can we get up there?"

He put up a hand and laughed. "Don't get ahead of yourself. We need to go over the mop-up procedure, so you know what you're doing. We need to set the crews and make sure everyone knows the safety plan. We're not rushing up a blazing mountain because your dog is up there. Priorities, right? You can't go looking in the woods for a dog when you've got work to do. The mop up zone is the safest place, but during a wildfire, that isn't saying much. It's dangerous work. You're clear on that?"

I must have looked uncertain.

"Listen kid, you're not going up there if you're going to be distracted. The fire has moved up the hill and the area we're looking at for mop-up is safe now, but things can change in an instant. You need to be where we expect you to be in case everyone has to bail out of there quickly. Got it?"

"Yes, sir." This wasn't good news. Of course, it made complete sense, but I needed to get Zuzu back. If I couldn't go hunting for her, I'd just have to hope when she heard her three whistles, she'd come to me as quickly as she was trained to. Three blasts meant race to me. Zuzu would leave whatever she was doing and come to sit in front of me to get a treat. I patted the dehydrated chicken hearts in the little bag in my pocket. They were Zuzu's favourite, the high value treat for after competitions when she needed her greatest focus.

By now, the room was full of people. Some were in gear with steel toed boots and hard-hats. I looked nervously, in case Brian was one of them.

Sara nudged me, "We'll head off. Call if you need us?"

"Yeah, thanks." I waved to Kieran as they left and focused on the meeting.

Some of the people were the officials from the Wildfire Service who were directing things, but most were members of the Volunteer Fire Department. The majority were young males, but I wasn't the only girl there. Two of the officials from the Wildfire Service were women. They spoke knowledgeably and concisely. One was a helicopter pilot. Three pilots were sharing the helicopter, working in eight-hour shifts around the clock. She explained one was flying, one was eating, and one was sleeping.

It sounded exhausting.

They distributed all the gear and divided us into teams of six to eight. We were assigned spots where the crew truck would drop us off. We were to work within sight of one another, so help was there in case of a sudden flare up. We had shovels, forestry rakes, a rakehoe tool called a McLeod for chopping and turning soil, firefighters' axes with a blade on one side and a pick called a mattock on the other, and each crew had a truck with a huge water tank in the box. There were two hoses attached to our tank.

I was nervous and excited. I had said I wanted to fight a fire, and now I was. There was no one around to tell me that I couldn't do it. The chief hadn't even blinked when I handed in my paperwork with the forged signatures. He didn't know my parents weren't around to sign. I knew under normal circumstances parents would have been expected to come to a meeting. They had gone when Brian volunteered during his last year of school. They knew what it was about. If they'd approved Brian, they couldn't very well not approve me, right?

Honestly, I was counting on the fact that by the time Mom found out I'd been in the fire zone, she wouldn't consider that small detail of parent permission. She'd probably blame Brian for not keeping me out of trouble. What a terrible role-model a firefighter big brother was. Ha.

I knew there wasn't a hope that she wouldn't find out that I'd joined. Laketon is small. No one gets secrets here for long. I just needed this secret to last until I had Zuzu back.

We piled into the crew pick-up and headed up the mountain.

~ 11 ~

It was eery driving up the mountain through the burnt-out area. All the underbrush was gone, and the evergreen forest was now full of blackened poles and stumps.

The smoke from the fire now burning several kilometres away still filled the air. Our boots kicked up ash as we climbed out of the trucks.

We were all wearing heavy pants, hard hats and steel toed boots to protect us from falling trees. Our job was to study the ground for smoking spots where the fire had moved into the root systems. Puffs of smoke meant chopping, raking, and shoveling to get past the organic soil to the mineral soil, and when we found whatever roots or mulch was smoulder, we turned it, raked it, and then the guy on the hose came by to spray it. Some areas, the ground was still green, but the fire had travelled along the crown of the trees. That was strange, too.

Perhaps the strangest thing was the silence. Usually when Zuzu and I were walking in the woods, it was full of rustlings in the underbrush, the chittering of squirrels, and the songs and squawks of birds. Now it was cracking and crunching, and the noise of the fire crew. It was like being on another planet.

Chris was in my crew. Our crew boss was Davis.

As our crew spread out with their chosen tools, combing the

ground for signs of hot spots, I looked around for signs of Zuzu, perhaps tufts of curly white hair caught on brambles or something. I didn't notice anything. "Davis?"

"Yeah?"

"Before I get to work, is it okay for me to whistle for my dog? Just in case she's around somewhere?"

He waved an arm, "Knock yourself out!"

The ash was thick, and puffs of smoke rose with every step. I coughed and my eyes burned, but I pursed my lips and whistled the three blasts that was the special signal for Zuzu to come running. "ZUZU!" I called as loudly as I could, and I whistled another three blasts before I was overcome with coughing again.

The other guys on the crew looked around, everyone pausing to listen, but there was nothing to indicate Zuzu was out there anywhere.

"Sorry kid," said Davis with a shake of his head. "Let's get to work now. You can try again later."

"Yeah. Thanks for letting me try."

Davis assigned me to a guy called Aaron, to learn how to use my Macleod.

Aaron showed me how to chop the ground with the sharp hoe side, then flip it to the rake side with its six fat finger-length tines. I could already tell I was going to have horrible blisters under my gloves tonight.

The crew spread out, raking, chopping. I got into the rhythm, scarcely looking up from the ground. Aaron and I together flipped over a smoking stump. A blaze burst out of it.

My heart thudded in my throat and I yelped.

"It's okay, kid. We'll get it. Come on. Kyle! Hose!"

Aaron chopped with the mattock side of his axe. I pulled away the pieces he broke off with my Macleod, raking and chopping. Kyle sprayed it down.

When Aaron slipped off his glove to test the temperature of the ground was satisfactorily cool, I slipped off mine, and reached into my waist pack for a water bottle.

I looked around for the rest of the crew. They were spread wide apart working in pairs. I couldn't see Chris or Davis, though.

I took another sip and then paused.

"Aaron? Do you hear something?"

Aaron stopped working and listened. There was the drone of the skimmer planes and the thump of helicopter blades overhead, on their way to drop water on the active part of the fire. There was a truck engine grumbling up the mountain. There was crackle of dried forest. "What?"

There was a high-pitched hiss.

"That," I whispered, my mouth suddenly dry.

There was barking.

"ZUZU!" I shouted, as I dropped my water bottle, grabbed my Macleod and tore up the hill toward the sound.

"Hey, kid! Wait!" Aaron called.

Then there was a scream.

~ 12 ~

I ran through the forest as Aaron hollered behind me. I didn't hear what he said. Obviously, I could guess that he wanted me to come back, but I wasn't going to stop, not when that barking had to be Zuzu, and it sounded like she was in trouble. My first duty was to my dog.

"Zuzu!" I shouted as I ran. "Zuzu, I'm coming!"

I tried to whistle, but I was breathing too hard to make any sounds. With every step puffs of ash rose around me, tickling my nostrils. Finally, I came up against a bare rock face. I had to stop to sneeze and cough.

"Zuzu?" I called. My voice echoed back from the cliff.

I looked around the blackened stumps and the sparse patches of undergrowth trying to get my bearings. I stood still, straining my ears for the sounds I'd heard. Hisses. Barks. A scream.

There was crackling

In the distance I could hear a rumble. Was it growling?

No. One of the water bombers on its way to the active fire line.

I stood there, panting and realized that having outrun Aaron and the crew, I was now alone in the forest.

Being with lots of other people in the forest gives security. Animals don't attack large noisy groups of humans.

I couldn't hear the rest of my fire crew.

I couldn't hear Zuzu's barks.

I couldn't hear whoever had screamed.

I couldn't hear birds.

Silence in a forest is bad.

Silence means something is lurking.

I stood absolutely still and felt like an idiot. I had just guaranteed that I'd never be allowed to be part of the Volunteer Fire Department when this was all over.

I had just increased the odds that some desperate animal would attack me.

The hair on the back of my neck rose and I knew my odds were running out.

I raised my McLeod tool and pivoted in a slow circle, trying to remember everything I'd heard about surviving wild animal attacks. Play dead with a grizzly but fight a black bear. Make yourself a big and tall as possible, and maintain eye contact with a wolf as you back away. Be big and arm yourself against a cougar, giving it an escape route. Be ready to show teeth and sound ferocious if it attacks. Be prepared to fight for your life. My heart was racing like drum solo. Stay calm, Delia. Figure out what it is.

I inhaled a deep breath as I scanned the blackened stumps and lump ground searching for the predator that I could feel was eyeing me.

There was a commotion behind me, and I raised my McLeod, spinning to face whatever was as I let out the best martial arts intimidation shout that I could manage, "YAAAAA!!!"

Chris stumbled into view, panting. "Delia!"

I stared at him, blinking with relief.

"What happened?" he gasped, bent over puffing from exertion, his hands grabbing at his knees. "Why did you scream?"

I shook my head, "I wasn't screaming."

"Then what was?" He didn't sound like he believed me.

"I don't know, but something is here. Can't you feel it?"

He shook his head, still bent over trying to catch his breath.

And then a rattle of pebbles behind me made me glance over my shoulder.

A blur of tawny brown as a huge cougar leapt from the rocks stretching right over me in a huge arc, its claws outstretched toward Chris.

Now I was the one who screamed. I shouted, "DUCK CHRIS!" as I ran forward with my McLeod raised. I was ready to swing at the cat like I was batting a ball to the outfield, but before I could get the rakehoe in motion, a snarling grey and black thing leapt over my head from the same rock the cougar had jumped from.

This is just not fair! I thought. *A cougar AND a wolf?!*

There was no time for Chris to do anything except drop to the ground and curl himself into a ball. He wrapped his hands in their thick leather gloves over the back of his neck beneath the brim of his hardhat. His tool belt protected his lower back. The grey wolf had its jaws on the cougar's neck as the animals snarled and writhed together.

The wolf's coat was strange, kind of curly. Its tail was an odd shape.

It wasn't a wolf.

It was Zuzu.

The animals twisted and the cougar was on top

I swung the McLeod, shouting curse words that would have got me grounded for a month.

~ 271 ~

Chris rolled away from the snarling animals.

My McLeod clanged on a rock beside them.

The cougar shook itself with a hissing snarl, and Zuzu released her grip, still growling.

I roared, "LEAVE MY DOG ALONE!" and lunged at the wild cat, slashing the McLeod back and forth ahead of me.

The cat flashed a look of absolute fury at me as I brought the McLeod down again, its sharp hoe edge slicing into the ground.

The cat's gold eyes stared at me.

Before I could lift the rakehoe up again, Aaron and the rest of the crew burst into our midst.

I shouted, "Watch out!"

Aaron spread his arms wide and started yelling, "BAD KITTY!" in a bellowing voice that probably carried into town.

The cougar's gaze darted frantically around at everyone, and then with another huge leap, it raced off up the mountain.

There was a dark streak as Zuzu went to follow it.

I whistled a blast louder than I had ever managed before. "STOP ZUZU!" I shouted with all the authority I could muster. " Come!"

And Zuzu spun around like it was a tight turn in agility class and she leapt into my arms.

~ 13 ~

I was lying on the ground laughing and squirming while I tried to avoid Zuzu's tongue as she covered me with kisses. "Good girl, Zuzu. Good girl." Forty-five pounds of flying poodle had flattened me, but I didn't care. My grin was so wide it hurt my face.

I wrenched myself up, rummaging in my pocket for the bag of dehydrated chicken heart. "What a good girl you are, Zuzu."

She gobbled the treats and sat in front of me, her tail moving so fast it was just a blur. Her coat was black from the ashes and rubbing up against blackened trees, but at the back of her neck, where her coat was thickest, there was a white gap.

Chris came up to me as I was probing it. "What happened there?"

"I think the cougar ripped out some of her hair. If she'd been a Labrador or something it would have gotten her neck."

"It just got a mouthful of fur?"

I nodded, tears flooding my eyes. I rummaged in my pack for the collar and leash I'd brought. "Oh, Zuzu! I almost lost you."

"Never mind her, you almost lost me!" said Chris. "If Zuzu hadn't leapt on that cougar's back, it would have killed me!" He shivered.

"Come on, everyone," called Aaron. "Is everyone all right? Chris? Did it get you?"

Chris straightened and looked his body up and down. He stretched his gloved arms forward and rotated them. "I don't feel... Oh. Ow."

There was a long line of red dripping down his shirt from a gash across his left bicep.

"Back to the truck everybody," said Aaron. "We need to get some first aid on that arm. Looks like you're going to need stitches, kid." He unclipped his phone and let the rest of the crew take the lead, as he took up the rear, telling whoever was on the other end of his phone that we had an injured crewman after a cougar attack.

As we walked through the forest, Zuzu walked in perfect heel position at my left side, her leash dangling in a gentle arc in front of me as I held it looped around my right wrist. She kept glancing up to my face, just like we were in a Rally Obedience trial.

"Yes!" I said, as I popped a piece of chicken heart into her mouth.

Zuzu wagged her tail.

Chris walked along beside us. "She's not growling at me anymore."

"I guess having saved you from a wildcat, she's decided she'll tolerate you."

"Good girl, Zuzu," he said, reaching out to pat her on the head.

Zuzu let out a faint rumble at the back of her throat, then glanced up at me and wagged her tail.

When we got back to the truck, everyone pulled out water bottles and sipped, while Aaron got out the first aid kit. He called

Chris over and poured a bottle of water over the gash.

Chris winced as the pink water puddled at his feet and dripped on his boots.

Aaron wrapped some gauze around Chris's arm and observed, "That could have been a lot worse."

"I know." Chris shuddered. "That was the most terrifying experience of my life."

"You were saved by a poodle, dude."

I stepped forward to hand Aaron a piece of medical tape to secure the gauze. "He was saved by one of the most intelligent members of canis domesticus," I rubbed Zuzu's back. "Consider yourself lucky, Chris."

"Considering how much she disliked me, I am surprised she didn't just let the cougar have me."

"Maybe she considers you family. She's allowed to fight with you, but no one else is?"

Chris laughed as a Wildfire Service truck rumbled up and stopped.

My heart dropped when my brother Brian stepped out of the cab. I turned my back to him. I reached into my pocket and pulled a mask over my mouth and nose. Covered with ash and masked, perhaps he wouldn't recognize me.

"You called in a cougar attack?" asked Brian as he strolled over to us.

Aaron nodded, "Relatively minor injury. It just got one good slash at him. A few stitches and he'll be fine.

"Lucky."

Brian glanced around the crew.

Beside me, Zuzu gave the happy whimper she had for greeting family and thumped her tail against my thigh.

"Zuzu?" Brian said, whirling to look at her. "Is that you?"

Zuzu's tail thumped harder.

"Oh, wow. Is Delia ever going to be happy to see you!"

"Delia's the one who found her!" interjected Chris before I could give him a warning glare.

Brian's brows dropped. "What do you mean?"

Aaron pointed, "That's Delia."

"What?" Brian roared.

Sheepishly, I pulled the mask down. "Hey."

Brian put his hands on his hips and glared at me. "You have some serious explaining to do young lady!" He sounded so exactly like our mother than I couldn't help bursting out laughing.

He narrowed his eyes even more. "Well?"

Before I could say anything, the claxon wail of an alarm blasted from my phone, and those of everyone else in the crew. It was the Emergency Alert notice.

~ 14 ~

Everyone pulled out a phone to read the announcement. I glanced around to see if there was more smoke coming from somewhere. Over my head the helicopter with its giant dangling orange bucket was flying up to the fire line.

I read the message: "The Evacuation Order for southeast Laketon is rescinded. Residents may return to their homes but should remain on Evacuation Alert at this time."

Chris whooped and punched the air.

Everyone began high fiving and cheering. Grinning ash blackened faces contrasted with their sparkling white teeth.

Our mop up block was finished for the day, so we piled into the pick-ups to head down the mountain.

"Delia!" called Brian, "You and Zuzu come with me."

"I want to stay with my crew!" I called back, over the heads of Aaron and Chris.

Aaron shook his head, "You might as well go get it over with. It's not a long drive back to town. If you don't show up, we'll send a search party."

I rolled my eyes. "Thanks a lot. This is my punishment for running off to find Zuzu, isn't it?"

Aaron laughed, "Might be. Let you brother have his say. We'll meet you for debrief at the hall."

Zuzu happily hopped up into the truck and sat looking out the window, her tongue lolling happily. She was absolutely filthy. I wondered how much shampoo it was going to take to return her coat to its usual white. I might have to shave out the traditional hair style that had saved her life today. I wrapped an arm around her shoulders and gave her a squeeze. "Love you, Zuzu."

She lapped a doggy kiss across my chin, as if to say, "I love you, too."

Brian didn't speak as he waited for all the crew trucks to pull out and start down the forestry service road. Once we were all moving, he said, "Care to explain what you're doing up here with a fire crew? I know Mom and Dad didn't give you permission."

"I had to find Zuzu. Pilots kept spotting her. I knew if I could get up there…" my voice trailed off.

Brian shifted gears. The truck bounced over ruts and rocks. "Wildfire fighting is not a pink job."

"Don't just parrot Mom and Dad. Think for yourself. You know women can fight wildfires. There are women on your crew. You know they are great at the job."

"Delia. They're not you."

"Fine. Then wildfire fighting is a pink job, because I did it. Jobs I do, are pink jobs, right? You should try mopping every floor in our house every weekend. It's much more work than mopping up forest fires." Which wasn't strictly true, but it was certainly a tedious chore without any glory.

Brian rolled his eyes, so he took my point. "You could have been hurt, and then what would Mom and Dad have said to me? I would have been in so much trouble for encouraging you."

I scoffed. "You never did anything remotely encouraging."

"They're going to say it's not women's work, Delia."

"Look, in just one day I worked with the mop-up crew. I put

out flare-ups. I found my dog. I defended a friend from a cougar."
My voice was getting louder with every sentence. "I'm not a total
screw up. In fact, I am practically a superhero!"

Brian sighed as we pulled into the Fire Hall parking lot.
"Fine. I get it. You are capable of fighting fires."

"Thank you." I got out of the cab, Zuzu's leash looped over
my wrist. She stood panting happily beside me as Brian joined
us. Like she hadn't just put me through a week of torture while
she played in the forest.

Brian threw an arm over my shoulder as we walked into the
building. "It's a big brother's job to look after his little sister. I
don't want to be a bad brother."

I wrapped my arm around his waist and gave it a squeeze. "I
love you, too."

He laughed and squeezed my shoulders.

The other crews were back, too, waiting for the day's debrief.
Everyone looked weary from the hard work, but I started to see
folks looking at me, and then murmuring. I looked around for
Chris. He was sitting in a chair against the wall, talking earnestly.

Chief Parker went to the microphone and everyone turned to
listen. He repeated the information about the Evacuation Order
being rescinded and there were more cheers and high fives around
the room.

"We do dangerous work," he said, expression grim, and we
have to be prepared for the unexpected, but there was a first today
in my career fighting fires in town or forest. Young Chris Turlock
there was jumped by a cougar today."

There was a gasp in the hall.

"He's lucky to have just received a good scratch. He'll have
a manly scar and a good tale to tell in the bar…" he coughed and

added, "when he's of legal age, of course.

Folks chuckled.

"In other good news, I know some of you have seen the posters around for Delia's missing dog. We're all thankful that Zuzu went after that cougar, and probably saved Chris's life. So let's here it for Zuzu!"

The crowd shouted "Hip, hip, hooray!" in an echoing chorus. I blushed. Zuzu wagged her tail.

The chief then carried on with the plans for the next day. I would be on the mop-up crew again, but I was leaving Zuzu in her kennel. No more bushwhacking for her.

A couple of paramedics came into the hall and went over to Chris.

Zuzu and I eased out of the crowd and joined them. "How's the arm?"

"Hey," said Chris grinning down at Zuzu. "It's my savior!"

Zuzu wagged her tail.

"I have to go so they can sterilize the wound and I can get stitches now," Chris told Zuzu. "But it'd be a lot worse without your help, girl, so don't think I don't appreciate your efforts."

Zuzu's tail wagged faster.

"Does it hurt?" I asked.

He grunted. "Like a mother."

Zuzu stretched her nose out to him and sniffed his knee.

Chris put out his fist for her to smell.

She pushed her head under his fist so he could scratch her head.

Chris laughed. "Look at that! We're friends now." He smiled over at me. "So, can I take you out for dinner sometime? Or to a dance at the Purple Barn?"

I smiled back but shook my head. "I'm not interested in a

romantic relationship Chris, I'm sorry. But like Zuzu, I'm happy to be your friend. Will that do?"

"I'm in the Friend Zone?" He made a melodramatic pout. "Harsh."

"Sorry." I shrugged. "Maybe someday, but not now. I've got other stuff on my mind these days."

Chris stood to follow the paramedics. "Well, at least I tried."

I waved as he headed out the door.

My phone buzzed in my pocket. There was a text from Mom. "Your brother says we should let you join the Volunteer Fire Department."

I typed back, "Yes! Please!"

I smiled over at Brian, who smiled back.

Yeah, it sucked that my parents still needed my brother's endorsement before they trusted that I could do a job traditionally associated with men, but at least it was a start.

Zuzu leaned her back against me. My best friend was home. Laketon was safe. I'd done my part to make it all happen.

It was enough.

I was enough.

Author's Note:

The summer of 2021 wildfires raged through the forests of British Columbia. Many of my friends and former students were on Evacuation Order or Evacuation Alert. Those of us in the interior spent weeks glued to the BC Wildfire Service updates, watching the weather, praying for rain.

I wrote *Wildfire!* in eight days under brown, ash-filled skies. I was half-way through the story when I saw a Facebook post about a missing standard poodle in the Monte Lake evacuation area. How astounding it was to see real life was imitating my art! I hope Jenna was eventually found safe, as Delia's Zuzu was.

SLB
Shuswap Lake, BC
August 2021

Acknowledgements:

Thanks to Anthony Smith and Ari Hickman for their feedback regarding wildfire fighting strategies, tools, and procedures.

Thanks to the BC Wildfire Service for protecting our communities, for their tools for tracking fires, and the detailed information they post about each Fire of Note, telling how each fire was being fought.